PORTRAITS
of LITTLE WOMEN
Ghostly Tales

Don't miss any of the
Portraits of Little Women

PORTRAITS
of LITTLE WOMEN

Ghostly Tales

Four Stories

Susan Beth Pfeffer

DELACORTE PRESS

Published by
Delacorte Press
an imprint of
Random House Children's Books
a division of Random House, Inc.
1540 Broadway
New York, New York 10036

Visit us on the Web! www.randomhouse.com/kids
Educators and librarians, for a variety of teaching tools, visit us at
www.randomhouse.com/teachers

Pfeffer, Susan Beth.
Ghostly tales : four stories / Susan Beth Pfeffer.
    p. cm. — (Portraits of little women)
    Summary: In four ghost stories, set in nineteenth-century
Concord, Massachusetts, each of the March sisters has a super-
natural encounter.
    ISBN 0-385-32741-2
    [1. Ghosts—Fiction. 2. Sisters—Fiction. 3. Family life—
New England—Fiction. 4. New England—Fiction.] I. Title.
PZ7.P44855 Gf 2000
[Fic]—dc21   00-024012

The text of this book is set in 13-point Cochin.
Book design by Patrice Sheridan

Manufactured in the United States of America

September 2000

10 9 8 7 6 5 4 3 2 1

BVG

FOR PEGGY RACZKOWSKI

CONTENTS

PROLOGUE

*N*o matter how many times Jo March made the climb into the attic and settled at the old table that served as her desk, she felt a sense of joy and anticipation. The table was littered with papers, some scribbled on, some blank and inviting. Beneath the papers, blotches of ink stained the tabletop as well as the chair she sat on. No one could ever accuse Jo of neatness.

But writing was her passion. In all kinds of weather (and the attic burned in summer and froze in winter), this was Jo's special refuge, the one place in a home filled with parents and sisters where she could be alone with her thoughts and her stories.

Today was no different. Her daily tasks had finally been completed, and now she was in the attic, her attic, with the empty pages staring at her, begging to be filled.

What should she write about? Another play, perhaps, filled with dukes and danger? Or one of the stories she'd begun putting down about her own life and the lives of her beloved family?

Jo opened the bottle of ink and carefully dipped her pen into it. Stories about her sisters, she decided, but not the everyday sorts of things. No, this time she'd write about herself, Meg, Beth, and Amy, and what they'd seen and known that no one else had ever seen, could ever know.

With a smile that lit up the dusty attic, Jo put pen to paper and began to scribble.

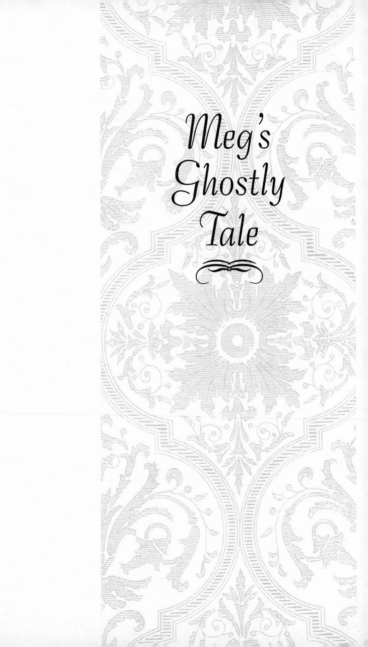

Meg's Ghostly Tale

CHAPTER 1

*M*eg wasn't sure whether it was the dull roar of thunder that woke her or the angry flash of lightning. But awaken she did. She listened for the comforting chatter downstairs of her parents and Hannah, the family housekeeper, but there was none. So she determined that they must already be asleep. It had to be the middle of the night.

Glancing over to the bed by the other wall, Meg saw her sister Jo, curled up and breathing deeply. Nothing woke Jo. Especially not a thunderstorm.

Another bolt of lightning lit up the room. For one terrifying second Meg could see everything as though it were daylight, except this light was hot and white and nearly blinding. It was followed by a roar of thunder so loud that Meg couldn't understand how anyone could sleep through it. She peeked over at Jo. The sky, no longer pitch black but almost purple from the rain clouds, cast a strange light onto her sister's face.

Can nothing wake Jo up? Meg asked herself as she huddled in her bed, dreading the next loud scream of thunder. When it came, she shook. She drew the covers over her head, but the flashes of lightning were so harsh and bright, not even a blanket could protect her eyes.

Meg counted between the lightning and the thunder. Her father had taught her that the longer the time between the two, the farther away the lightning was. The first few times, she counted as high as ten. But then they grew closer and closer together, and the thunder gained in intensity.

When a clap of thunder sounded at almost the exact same moment as the lightning flash,

Meg screamed. No one heard her, though. Not even Jo.

"Jo," Meg whispered, fully aware that if Jo could sleep through a thunderstorm, she was unlikely to wake up at the sound of her whispered name. "Jo?"

No response.

Another bolt of lightning was followed by an explosion of thunder. Meg couldn't stand it anymore. She raced from her bed and jumped onto Jo's.

"Jo," she said, "wake up."

Perhaps it was the thunder, perhaps it was Meg's leaping onto her bed, or maybe it was the shove that Meg gave her, but Jo finally opened her eyes. "Wha . . . ," she muttered.

"I want to sleep in your bed," Meg whispered. "Just go back to sleep."

"I am asleep," Jo said, but then she opened her eyes fully and looked at her sister. "Thunderstorm, hmm?" she said.

"I simply got lonely," Meg said, but the lightning and thunder made her shake with fear.

Jo laughed. "You're a bigger baby than Amy sometimes," she said, referring to the youngest of their sisters. "Thunder and lightning don't bother her."

"Amy's too young to know what to be scared of," Meg said.

"I must still be asleep," Jo said. "I have no idea what you just said."

"It doesn't matter," Meg replied. "Just go back to sleep."

"With you shaking and screaming?" Jo asked, rubbing her eyes and sitting up in bed. "How am I supposed to sleep through that?"

Meg thought about remarking that Jo had slept through just that and more, but there was no point. Instead she curled up in a ball and tried to pretend a thunderstorm wasn't right outside her window.

"There's nothing to be scared of," Jo said. "It's just a part of nature. Snowstorms are a part of nature, and you're not scared of them, are you, Meg?"

"Snowstorms are quiet," Meg mumbled. "They don't flash about."

"Snowstorms can so be noisy when the wind howls," Jo said. "And the white of the snow can be blinding as well. But you love snowstorms, Meg. Marmee is always calling you in from one, and you stay outside as long as you can, dancing away and trying to catch snowflakes on your tongue."

There was another flash of lightning. Meg closed her eyes and counted again. This time she reached the number six before the sound of the thunder filled the night. *Good. The storm must be passing,* she thought. But the next lightning flash was so bright that she quickly got under the covers with Jo.

"I don't see why there has to be thunder and lightning," Meg said. "I think the world would be just as fine a place without them."

"Oh, no," said Jo. "Think how hot it was yesterday, and how sticky. The storm will clear the air and make it bright and comfortable again."

"In that case, a snowstorm would do just as well," said Meg.

Jo laughed. "A snowstorm in August," she replied. "That truly would be frightening."

"I'm not really afraid of thunder and lightning," Meg said, pulling the covers up to her chin. "It's just that they startle me so."

"Of course," Jo said. "No one likes to be startled. Except perhaps in one of my plays. Remember how the audience never expected the Count of Burgundy to reappear after he had seemingly drowned in the previous act?"

Another burst of lightning lit the sky. This time Meg counted to twelve. The storm was definitely moving away, off to bother someone else.

"I think maybe I'll go back to my own bed," Meg said. "I'll sleep better there."

"I'll miss you," Jo said.

Meg smiled. She got out from under Jo's covers and crossed the three feet to her own bed. The next flash of lightning hardly even lit up the room, and the thunder sounded many miles away.

Jo fell back asleep almost immediately. It took Meg a little bit longer.

*E*ven though it was summertime, Meg and her sisters still had tasks to do about the house. Little Amy was expected to pitch in also, although of all of them she was the most likely to complain about it.

Jo grumbled too, especially on hot summer days when she longed to be outside running around or upstairs in her beloved attic working on another of her plays. Beth never complained, because it wasn't in her nature to. Only Meg enjoyed the housework and did all that was asked of her with a genuine smile. She would have done Amy's work as well, except Marmee had explained once that they shouldn't spoil her.

Amy clearly wouldn't have minded being spoiled, and she sighed deeply as she dusted the lower shelves with an old rag. "Someday I shall be so rich, I'll have a dozen servants to do my dusting for me," she declared.

"Just your dusting?" Beth asked. She reached for the middle shelves, which were a bit too high for Amy to get to.

"Just for dusting," Amy said. "And a dozen servants for sweeping and another dozen for mopping."

"How many cooks?" Jo asked from her perch on the footstool, where she was dusting the top shelves.

"Two dozen," replied Amy.

"I'm sure none of them would be as good a cook as Hannah," Beth said loyally.

"Hannah will teach them, then," said Amy.

"And will you be the one to teach them how to dust?" Meg said, laughing. "Really, Amy, I think you leave more dust on the shelves than on the rag."

"This rag is very dirty," Amy said, making a face. "Besides, a true lady should never have to touch anything soiled."

"Marmee says a true lady is never afraid of working or getting her hands dirty," Beth announced.

"I'm not afraid," Amy said. "I just don't want to."

"Are you afraid of getting *your* hands dirty?" Jo asked Meg. "Or are you only afraid of thunder and lightning?"

"I'm not afraid of any such thing!" Meg cried. "Honestly, Jo, do you have to bring that up?"

"What?" Amy asked. "What is Jo bringing up?"

"Amy slept through the storm," Beth said. "It woke me, though. I don't blame you, Meg, if it frightened you. It was so close by."

Meg didn't know which she disliked more, Jo's superior air or Beth's kindhearted pity. Meg was ten years old, and as the oldest sister,

14

she expected to be treated with a little respect. "I wasn't scared," she said. "The storm woke me, that's all."

Jo laughed. "You should have seen her," she said to her younger sisters. "Meg was shaking so hard, I thought my bed would collapse."

"That's not true!" Meg cried, but before she had a chance to defend herself, Marmee rushed into the room.

"Girls, put your cleaning aside. Aunt March's carriage is coming this way. She must have decided to pay us a call this morning."

Meg sighed at the thought of an unexpected visit from Aunt March. Then Jo sighed, and finally Beth. The three sisters waited for a sigh from Amy, but there was none. Instead she smiled.

"Oh, good," Amy said. "I was getting so tired of dusting."

Even Jo preferred cleaning to a visit from Aunt March, Meg knew, but the girls had no choice. They raced to the kitchen with their supplies and washed their hands. But they remained in their work clothes, and Meg could see the smudges on her sisters' faces. There was no time for a complete cleaning, and certainly none to change into their better dresses. Aunt March would simply have to see them as they were.

Which Aunt March promptly did. "What is the matter with these girls?" she asked almost as soon as she entered the house. "They look like street urchins, all covered in dirt and their dresses hardly better than rags."

"We've been dusting, Aunt March," Meg said, not sure if that was an explanation or an apology.

"Dusting?" Aunt March said, looking horrified.

"Yes, dusting," Marmee said. "I have often told the girls that a true lady should never be afraid of work or of getting dirty."

"A true lady should never have the need to work or get dirty," Aunt March replied. "Except perhaps during a war, and I don't think we have one of those in Concord at the moment."

"Really, Aunt March," Marmee said. "You

know how pleased I am when you come call-ing, but if we don't know to expect you, we must do what has to get done. The house is in need of a thorough cleaning, and I'm pleased to say my girls are strong enough and good enough to help out."

"Have you ever dusted, Aunt March?" Amy asked.

Meg held her breath. Amy was Aunt March's favorite, but there was no way of knowing what would amuse the elderly widow and what would offend her.

This time Aunt March was amused. She looked down at Amy and laughed. "Gracious, no, child," she said. "I think my mother would have died before she'd let me dust. Still, times are different, and your mother has a point. We must all be prepared for what life will hand us, and while I'm confident, Amy, that you'll make a good marriage and have servants to do the dusting and cleaning in your house, I can-not be so sure about your sisters. So if they dust, then you must as well."

Amy nodded. "Life is unfair," she said.

Aunt March laughed all the louder. "From the mouths of babes," she said. "Well, now that I'm here, am I not to be invited into the parlor and offered something cool to drink?"

"Of course, Aunt March," Marmee said. "Bethy, dear, go to the kitchen and see what there is for Aunt March."

Beth scampered out of the hallway as Meg and her sisters followed Marmee and Aunt March into the parlor.

"That was quite a storm we had last night," Aunt March said. "It roused me from a heavy sleep and kept me awake for a long time."

"It woke me too, Aunt March," Meg said.

"Me too," Jo said. "For Meg woke me up to keep her company."

"I have never cared for thunderstorms," Aunt March declared. "So noisy." She scowled, which Meg took to mean that thunderstorms were like dusting, something a true lady shouldn't be involved with.

"I like thunderstorms," Marmee declared. "I like their drama, their excitement."

Aunt March looked disapprovingly at her. "I trust you've taught your daughters the danger of a storm," she said. "People struck by lightning often die, you know. And lightning can cause fires as well."

"Of course I've taught them all that," Marmee said. "But I still enjoy thunderstorms from the safety of my own home."

"Even indoors you may not be completely safe," Aunt March said. "You must have been told the story of the family whose house caught fire from a flash of lightning. It happened forty years ago, I think, shortly after I married Mr. March. Terrible thing it was, the young mother dying that way."

"I know the story," Marmee said. "But I would prefer it if the girls didn't just yet."

"No, of course not," Aunt March said. "Still, it pays to be careful, girls. Lightning can kill."

"Even a true lady?" Amy asked.

Aunt March laughed so loudly, she rivaled

thunder. "Even a true lady," she said. "If she should happen to find herself in the wrong place at the wrong time."

Meg vowed she would never find herself in the wrong place at the wrong time—ever.

CHAPTER 3

"*M*armee, can we go berry picking?" Jo asked later that afternoon.

"Oh, yes, Marmee," Meg said. "Please. The raspberries were almost ripe last week. I'm sure we could bring back buckets of them today."

"I wish you had thought of it earlier," Marmee said.

"We were busy earlier," Amy said. "Dusting."

"And being polite to Aunt March," Jo said. "Then we had to finish our chores, and then Mrs. Williams came over and brought all that mending for the poor. We've been cooped up all day, and there isn't that much of summer left."

Marmee shook her head, but Meg could tell from her smile that berry picking was in their future. "What tragic lives my daughters lead," Marmee said. "Helping their mother, helping the poor. No wonder they have to go outside and pick berries."

"You mean we may?" Beth asked.

"Yes, you may," Marmee replied. "Your father has a meeting tonight, and he won't be home for supper. The sun stays out until well past eight, so it should be light for quite a long time now. Get home before dark, and I'll have Hannah prepare something cold for us to eat. If you pick enough berries, we'll make preserves of them. Won't they taste good in front of the fire this winter?"

On that warm summer day, Meg found it hard to believe there would ever be a winter. But she knew there was bound to be, and decided to pick not one but two full buckets of berries.

The girls changed back into their house-cleaning clothes, since berry picking always meant berry eating and the juice easily dribbled onto their dresses. Then they ran to the kitchen, where Hannah had assembled a variety of bowls and pails for them. Amy and Beth each took a small pail. Jo grabbed the two biggest bowls, vowing she'd be careful and not spill a single berry on the walk home. That left Meg one pail and one bowl. They wouldn't have been her first choice, especially since the bowl was chipped and not very pretty. But no one would see them, she told herself, and even a chipped bowl could hold a lot of raspberries.

"Now, be careful in the woods," Marmee said to them. "And come home well before dark."

"Don't worry, Marmee," Jo said. "Meg is scared of the dark. We'll be back way before then."

"I am not scared of the dark," Meg said. "Marmee, tell Jo to stop teasing me."

"Tell me yourself," Jo said.

"Girls, please behave." Marmee shook her

head. "Berry picking should be fun, and it won't be if you keep teasing each other."

"I'll be good, I promise," Jo said. "I'm sorry, Meg. I know you're not scared of the dark."

"Thank you," Meg said. She wished she'd slept through the storm the night before, or at least hadn't awakened Jo.

"Don't stay out too late," Marmee called after the girls as they began skipping down the road.

"We have to go through the woods," Meg told her sisters a while later. "Then we go a little ways in, until we reach the spot where there's an enormous berry patch. I discovered it last summer, and I've been checking on it almost every day now, waiting for the berries to ripen. You have to get to them before the birds do, or else they'll eat them all."

"Do you think we'll find enough to make preserves?" Beth asked. "Father loves them so."

"We may find enough, but we have to be careful not to eat them all off the bush," Meg said. "Especially you, Jo."

"I'll be good," Jo promised, but Meg knew she'd have to keep an eye on her. Jo loved raspberries and would gladly eat three bowls and three pails all by herself.

"The woods scare me sometimes," Beth said as they came to a wooded area and started down a path, trying hard to keep the branches from tearing at their clothing.

"I love the woods," Jo said. "So dark and mysterious."

"I don't think true ladies live in the woods," Amy said.

"What about the mother who died?" Beth asked. "Was she a true lady?"

"The one Aunt March started telling us about?" Jo said. "I know the whole story."

"How?" Meg asked. "It happened forty years ago."

"I heard it from one of the schoolboys," Jo said. "His older brother loved telling him the story late at night just to scare him. It happened right in these woods."

"Tell us, Jo," Amy said.

Meg wasn't at all sure she wanted to hear the

story, but she didn't dare ask Jo to stop for fear of more teasing.

"There were a father and a mother and two children," Jo began. "The father was away from home. He'd gone on a hunting trip. They had a little patch of land on which to grow their vegetables, and they ate those and what the father could catch."

"They must not have been very rich," Amy said.

"No, but they loved each other, and the parents were trying to make a good life for their children," Jo said. "Marmee always says that's what's important. Anyway, the father was gone, and the mother was alone with her two little children. It was a hot summer's night, just like last night. And just like last night, there was a fierce storm. But it had been a dry summer, and when the lightning hit a tree by the cabin, it caught fire. Soon the cabin was ablaze as well."

Meg yearned for Jo to stop, but she knew Jo wouldn't. So she walked a little farther ahead, hoping not to hear every detail, but she did anyway.

"The mother woke up to find the cabin on fire," Jo continued. "The place was filled with smoke, and she couldn't see two inches in front of her. She could hear her baby crying, so she grabbed it from its cradle and ran outside. Then she realized she hadn't seen her other child, a little boy not four years old. She ran back to the house crying for the boy, but once she got in, the house burst into flames. The mother perished trying to save her son."

"How awful," Beth said.

"It's worse than that." Jo cleared her throat. "The next day the father came back with a wild pheasant he had caught. But he found his home burned to the ground. Nothing remained but a few charred pots and pans."

"What became of the baby?" Beth asked, and in spite of herself, Meg lingered to be sure she heard the answer.

"Did wolves carry it off?" Amy asked. "The way they did in one of your plays, Jo?"

"That was what the father feared," Jo said. "Or that the baby and the little boy had perished in the fire along with their mother. But as he walked through the woods he found the baby and the little boy huddled together for warmth."

"I thought the boy had died in the fire," Meg said.

Jo shook her head. "He had gone out of the cabin to relieve himself," she said, "before the fire began. His mother ran in to save him, not knowing he was safely out of the house. She died for no reason."

"That's horrible," Meg said.

"They say she haunts the woods still," Jo said. "That on some nights what you think is the wind howling is that poor mother crying out for her boy, not knowing to this day that he is still alive and never had been in danger."

"Of course she doesn't know," Amy said. "She's dead. That's a silly story, Jo. Did you make it up yourself?"

"I did not," Jo said. "All the boys in Concord know that story. The only reason the girls don't is because the boys think we're too fragile. Boys!"

"I don't think it's a really good story," Beth

said. "It's a sad one, and it makes me unhappy to be in the woods where it happened. Do we have much farther to go, Meg, before we reach the patch?"

"I hope not," Amy said. "I'm hungry."

"How can you be hungry?" Jo asked. "I saw you eat an apple no more than an hour ago."

"I can't help it, I'm hungry," Amy whined. "And if we go berry picking now, we won't have supper for hours and hours. I shall be so weak with hunger, you'll have to carry me home."

"You can be such a crybaby, Amy," Jo said. "We're here to pick berries. You can eat some while you pick, and then you won't be hungry anymore."

"I want to go home too," Beth said. "I'm sorry, Jo, but your story upset me. I want to see Marmee and make sure she's all right. I want to check on Hannah, too, and my kittens and my dollies."

"Why shouldn't they be all right?" Jo asked. "There isn't a cloud in the sky. There's nothing to worry about."

Amy began to cry. "I want to go home," she said. "I don't want to be in these woods anymore."

"Please," Beth said. "I want to go back too."

"Then go," Jo said. "And let us big girls pick berries without you."

"We can't send them home by themselves," Meg said. "One of us will have to take them back, Jo."

"Then you take them," Jo said. "You're probably frightened by my story as well."

"That's not fair," Meg said. "Besides, I'm the only one who knows where the berry patch is. You take Beth and Amy home, Jo, and I'll check on the patch and pick enough berries for supper tonight. Tomorrow morning we'll all come back and pick bushels of berries for preserves."

"Oh, all right," Jo grumbled. "Just don't eat all the berries yourself, Meg."

"I won't. Now hurry home, and tell Marmee I'll be back in an hour."

Jo looked unhappy, but at least her temper didn't flare. Instead she turned around and began the walk home with Amy on one side and Beth on the other. Soon Meg heard Jo's familiar whistling. Meg didn't approve of such conduct, but she wasn't about to scold. It was too delightful knowing she would have some quiet time to herself to worry about Jo's boyish behavior.

CHAPTER 4

Meg loved being in the woods. She loved the quiet of the forest, the only sounds coming from the singing birds and the buzzing insects. She also loved the scampering squirrels and catching glimpses of deer.

As she made her way deeper into the woods, she found her berry patch. The berries were heavy on the bushes, and after looking around, Meg chose one that was so filled with ripe raspberries that she knew she could eat her fill and still have enough to take home.

She lost herself in the job, finishing one bush

and beginning on another. All the while she hummed and dreamed of the man she'd some-day marry and the children who would call her Mother. She was so involved with her thoughts that the first drops of rain startled her.

Meg looked up at the sky and discovered it was dark as midnight. In the distance she saw a flash of lightning.

Immediately she decided to make her way home, but the rain started coming down hard. It was difficult to see. She wasn't sure which was the path she always followed.

Turning one way and then another, Meg only became more confused. She was sure of just one thing: The woods were a dangerous place to be in a thunderstorm. And having lost her sense of direction, she grew more and more frightened. She knew the worst of the storm was yet to come.

"Don't drop any berries," she whispered, as though by saving the berries she would save herself. It was hard to run without dropping any berries from the pail and the bowl. She nearly tripped more than once.

33

The trees seemed to grow larger, the spaces between them shrank into nothingness, and Meg knew she was lost. Lost in the woods. And if the lightning didn't find her, a wolf surely would.

"Oh, Marmee!" she cried, knowing no one could hear her, no one could save her.

"Over here! Follow the lantern!"

Had Meg imagined it, or was someone calling to her? She looked around, and in the distance she made out the dim glow of a lantern flame.

Meg didn't know who could be in the woods, but at this point she no longer cared. The intensity of the lightning made her run toward the flame.

It was hard to see through the pelting rain, but the flame grew brighter, and Meg knew she was nearing safety. When she got within a hundred feet of the lantern, she could see a small cabin filled with friendly voices and cheering smells.

A woman was standing by the doorway, holding the lantern. "You poor child," the

woman said, ushering Meg in. "You're drenched."

"The rain caught me by surprise," Meg said, clutching the bowl and the pail.

"Of course it did," the woman said. "We've had such a dry summer. I know the farmers need the rain for the crops, but I must admit lightning frightens me."

"It frightens me as well," Meg said. She could see by the light of the lantern that the cabin she had entered was hardly more than a shack. Still, there was a small stove, and on it was a kettle. In one corner Meg spotted a cradle with a sleeping baby.

"That's Jedediah," the woman said, smiling at Meg. "He can sleep through anything. Isaiah, though, wakes up easily. Don't you, Isaiah?"

Meg saw a little boy sitting on the floor, playing with a branch that had been whittled into the shape of a musket. "Bang, bang," he said, pointing his weapon at Meg.

The woman laughed. "It's not good manners to shoot at strangers," she said. "You poor child. Soaking wet, and now attacked by a vicious hunter."

"Is that me, Mama?" Isaiah asked. "Am I the vicious hunter?"

"I don't see anyone else in this cabin," his mother said.

Isaiah looked quite pleased with himself. "What's vicious?" he asked.

"I'll tell you later." The woman smiled. "Now we have to dry this poor girl off and give her some hot tea to drink."

"Thank you," Meg said. "This is very kind of you."

"I'm glad of the company. It can get awfully lonely in these woods, even with two babes. A visitor makes for a nice diversion. I only wish you could be more comfortable."

"I'm fine, really," Meg said.

The woman pointed to the table. "Put that pail and bowl down. It looks as though you've been berrying."

"I have been," Meg said. "But the storm hit."

"Take this," the woman said, handing Meg

an old wool jacket. "Put it over you. And dry your hair off with this." She handed Meg an old piece of flannel, which Meg rubbed over her face, hands, and hair.

"There, that's better," the woman said. "Now we'll share that cup of tea, and by the time we're through, I'm sure the rain will have stopped."

"Good," Meg said. "I really should get home as soon as possible. My mother is probably worried about me."

"Tea first, then home," the woman said. She poured the tea into two battered tin cups. Just the feel of the warm cup in Meg's hands made her feel safer.

"Do you live nearby?" the woman asked. "I don't remember seeing you in these woods."

"I live closer to Concord," Meg said. "My name is Meg March."

"I've met the Marches," the woman said. "Fine people. I don't get into town much. It's too long a journey with these little ones. But when I do, the sights I see! Concord grows bigger every time I visit."

"Do you think Isaiah will go to school there?" Meg asked. "The school is very good, and in the winter he could board in town so he wouldn't have to make the long walk through the woods."

"Child, we live one season at a time here," the woman said. "Isaiah won't need any real schooling for two years or more, and I can't begin to guess what our lives will be like then. Lord willing, we'll have our health, and that's a lot more important than any schooling."

Meg nodded. She knew health was more important than schooling, but she suspected schooling was more important to her than it was to this kind woman who'd given her shelter from the storm.

The woman looked at her and laughed. "You must think us savages," she said. "Alone in the woods with no man to protect us. My husband is away for a few days. He'll be back soon enough, and when he comes, he'll bring us food for the fall. Then he'll go out again and trap animals for their fur. He'll carry the pelts to town, where he'll trade them for flour and salt and all the supplies we'll need for the winter."

"I want to be a trapper too," Isaiah said.

"You will be, son," his mother said. "So will Jedediah someday. And if the Lord sees fit to bless me with a daughter, she'll learn to grow food from seed and to skin an animal and to make a little cabin in the woods feel like a rich man's mansion."

"I think your home is much nicer than a mansion," Meg said, ashamed of what she'd been thinking earlier. "Of course, I haven't been in a lot of mansions, but they can't be as nice or as friendly as this house."

"Bless you, child. I certainly do try," the woman said. "Would you like some more tea? It seems to have put the color back in your cheeks."

Meg would have enjoyed another cup, but she suspected even a single cup of tea was a sacrifice for her hostess. "Thank you," she said instead. "I think the storm is passing, and I really should be getting home."

"All good things must come to an end," the

woman said. "I've enjoyed our little visit. Maybe you could come back someday?"

"I'd like to," Meg said. "I'll bring my mother with me next time."

"A fine young lady like Mrs. March?" the woman said, and roared with laughter. "In a shanty like this one?"

"My mother doesn't put on airs," Meg said. "Truly she doesn't."

"You know her better than I do," the woman said. "Here, take that old coat off you. Thanks again for your visit."

"Thank *you*," Meg said, handing the coat back. "Good-bye, Isaiah," she said. "Good-bye, Jedediah."

"Bang, bang," Isaiah said.

The woman opened the cabin door. "Make it home safely, now."

"I will," Meg said. "I'll be fine. It's only raining very lightly. The storm is heading away." She curtseyed to the lady, waved to Isaiah, and began the walk back through the woods to the safety of her home.

*M*eg had gone only a short way when lightning flashed in the distance. Suddenly she remembered the berries. She'd left them at the cabin.

"Oh, no," she said out loud. She decided to go home and return for them the next day.

But she thought about the woman, alone with the two young children, and how the berries would be sure to be a temptation. Isaiah would no doubt want to eat them, and his mother might not have the heart to tell him he couldn't.

Meg certainly didn't mind sharing the berries. The patch they came from was no more hers than anyone else's. She had merely found it before someone else had. And there were loads of berries left for her and her sisters to pick the next day.

Still, Meg turned around and headed back to the cabin. *I'll tell the nice lady to keep the berries but to give me the bowl and the pail*, she thought. She was sure that was what Marmee would tell her to do.

Another flash of lightning almost made her reconsider, but the thunder was distant and the rain suddenly stopped. As Meg bravely retraced her steps she saw a hint of blue in the sky and enough sun that she felt sure she was safe and doing the right thing.

But no matter how long she looked, Meg couldn't find the cabin. She wasn't about to give up, though. Even a chipped bowl was valuable to the Marches, and Hannah would scold her roundly if she lost a good pail.

Meg made her way back to the berry patch and tried to figure out which route to take. The woods looked different now that it had ceased raining. The trees were no longer so large, and it was easy to see her way through them.

The cabin had to be here somewhere. She wondered if Marmee knew where the woman lived, and if she would be willing to pay her a call in the future. Meg wanted to prove to the woman that her mother wasn't the sort of lady who looked down on hardworking folk who were fighting to survive.

Meg continued her search, and she finally spotted a small clearing in the woods. *That must be their garden*, she told herself, and began walking faster. There was no lantern to guide her this time, but Meg was certain she was on the right path as the clearing grew nearer.

But when Meg reached the clearing, there was no cabin in sight, only some wild bushes and weedy plants.

Bewildered, Meg turned to leave, and her foot kicked something. She bent down and found an old teakettle, blackened from a long-ago fire and rusted from years in the rain.

Meg picked up the kettle, then dropped it as though it had scalded her. But it hadn't been hot. Meg had simply had a shock of recognition. As she willed herself to look about her on the ground, she noticed the gleam of metal. It was the light reflecting off a metal pail.

"No," she said out loud. "It can't be." But next to the pail was an old, chipped bowl. Both the pail and bowl were filled with raspberries washed clean by rain.

Meg suddenly recalled how the woman had referred to Mrs. March, and she realized the woman hadn't meant Marmee at all. She had been speaking of Aunt March, but from forty years before. Because forty years before, there had been a fire in a cabin in the woods, and the mother of two little boys had died a horrible death.

As Meg bent down to pick up the bowl and the pail of raspberries, she saw yet another glint, this one of a lantern, a candle still in it. She touched the wick and felt a little warmth from it.

If there was an explanation, Meg didn't care to know what it was. She began the long run home, berries flying from the bowl and from the pail. Meg flew too, chased by the sound of the wind, a howling wind that seemed to be crying, "Isaiah, Isaiah," in the twilight of the forest.

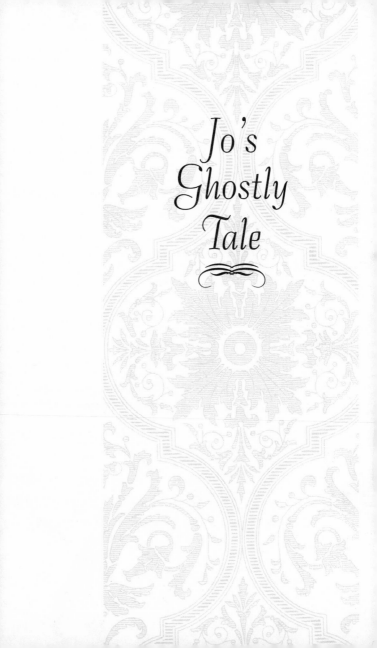

Jo's
Ghostly
Tale

CHAPTER 1

"You are so fortunate," Amy said to Jo as all four March girls hovered in Jo and Meg's bedroom. "How I wish I were the one getting to go."

"I wish you were the one too," Jo replied. "Meg, what shall I do? I've scorched my best dress, lost half my hair ribbons, and can't seem to find my right shoe."

"You can have my hair ribbons, Jo," Beth said.

"And your right shoe is under my bed," Meg said, lying on the floor and pulling the shoe out.

"That solves shoes and hair ribbons," Jo

said. "I suppose I should simply not worry about my dress."

"Marmee did a good job patching it," Beth said. "No one will notice, I'm sure."

"Pauline won't," Amy said.

Meg, Jo, and Beth all stared at Amy.

"Well, she won't," Amy said.

"I'm going to assume you mean Pauline Wheeler is such a lady she would never notice anything as unimportant as a patch on a dress," Meg said. "That is what you meant, isn't it, Amy?"

"Pauline is a lady," Amy said. "But she's also blind, and we all know it. Jo never would have met her if she hadn't been blind."

Jo thought about it. Pauline had been visiting her grandparents in Concord when she and Jo met. Pauline had no friends because she'd been kept isolated by her parents, who were shamed by their daughter's blindness.

Jo hadn't liked Pauline at first, but the two girls had been caught in a blizzard together, and Pauline had proved herself brave and resourceful. Ever since, Jo had learned to respect and like her.

Now Pauline had begun attending the Perkins School in Boston, a school devoted to educating the blind. Pauline often dictated letters, so she and Jo had corresponded with each other many times. Over the months, Jo's respect and affection for her friend had steadily grown.

Still, Jo had been surprised when Pauline had written to invite her for a visit at her mother's father's home. Pauline's parents were abroad, trying to find fine husbands for her older sisters. Instead of spending the summer with her Concord grandparents, Pauline was visiting the other side of her family, which consisted only of a widowed grandfather.

Pauline's letter had been guarded, but Jo could tell she needed a visit from her friend. And even though Jo would have been just as happy at home, writing in the attic, playing with her sisters, and enjoying the freedom from schoolwork and the pleasures of warm summer days, she knew Pauline needed her. She had to go.

"It's not polite to mention Pauline's affliction," Meg said to Amy.

"But it's true," Amy said. "Father always says we should speak the truth."

"Only if the truth needs to be spoken," Meg said. "Isn't that so, Jo?"

Jo was no longer paying attention. She was looking at the bag she had borrowed from her father for this visit and the clothing she'd packed. "I could use new handkerchiefs," she said. "And new stockings, and new undergarments." She sighed. "I could use new everything. Ink and dirt seem to get on everything I own."

"That's because you're careless," Meg said.

"Jo is careless, and Amy is rude," Beth said. "What does that make me, Meg?"

"Foolish to ask such a question," Jo said. "For Meg could find a weakness even in you, Bethy."

"I know my weaknesses well enough," Beth said. "I should never have the courage to visit

strangers. I think you're so brave, Jo, to visit Pauline at her grandfather's."

"Even Aunt March thinks Mr. Dodge is a difficult man," Meg said. "And no one is more difficult than Aunt March."

"But he's rich," Amy said. "His home is certain to be filled with beautiful things. He'll have maids and butlers and carriages and splendid horses, and hothouses filled with roses and orchids. There'll be balls with women in flowing gowns and handsome gentlemen. Dukes and princes. Diamonds, emeralds. You'll get to see it all."

"That isn't why Jo is visiting," Beth said. "She's visiting because Pauline needs her company."

Jo turned to Beth and smiled. "You're right," she said. "The way you always are, Bethy. Pauline needs me, and she doesn't care if my dresses are patched."

"Still, if you have to go where you're needed," Amy said, "it's so much nicer to be needed by rich people."

"Amy!" Meg cried. But Jo understood Amy's reasoning even if she didn't share her sister's feelings. She would have much preferred that Pauline be just a bit less rich, and that dukes, princes, or other titled people wouldn't be around to notice the patches on her dress.

CHAPTER 2

*J*o ate breakfast early the next morning, with only Father and Marmee for company. It had been arranged that Mr. Dodge's carriage would pick her up at seven, since the drive to his house would take the entire day.

Jo was eager to see the world, but no matter how wealthy Mr. Dodge might be and how elegant his carriage, she knew it would be a long and wearying journey.

Hannah had packed apples, bread, and cheese for Jo to eat, although there would be stops at inns on the way. Still, it made Jo feel better to have something from home with her.

56

The liveryman with the carriage arrived, and Jo hugged her parents good-bye.

"Do us proud," Father said. "Be the fine girl we know you to be, Jo."

"And enjoy yourself," Marmee said. "Give our love to Pauline, and know you'll be in our thoughts and prayers every moment, my darling Jo."

Jo smiled bravely at her parents. She suddenly felt as though she were being driven to her doom and not to a visit with a friend.

"Good-bye, Jo!"

Jo looked up. Her three sisters were waving to her from her bedroom window. Just seeing them brightened her mood.

"Tell Pauline we miss her!" Beth cried.

"Remember everything you see," Meg said.

"Find me a prince!" Amy shouted.

The sisters laughed, and Jo laughed with them. The next two weeks surely wouldn't be a trial, and besides, she had such wonderful parents and sisters to come home to.

The roads were rough and the journey long, but after the stop for lunch Jo convinced the liveryman that she would be far more

comfortable riding in the front with him. It was cooler sitting outside, and the view far better.

Jo tried to make conversation, but the liveryman didn't seem at ease talking with her. So Jo entertained herself by looking at countryside she'd never seen before. It was very lush, with houses scattered about. The longer they drove, the wilder the landscape became, and the jollier the response of the people as they rode by.

Jo waved to them all, pleased when they waved back. The people were so friendly, she decided, that Mr. Dodge was sure to be as well. How bad could he be, after all, if he'd agreed to Jo's visit?

Jo's mood brightened, and her excitement grew. She was indeed fortunate to have Pauline for a friend, as well as an opportunity to visit a new place and meet new people. Perhaps she'd have an exciting adventure. That certainly would be something to tell her sisters when she returned home.

"This is the path to the Dodge house," the liveryman announced many hours later. Jo had become concerned that they wouldn't arrive before dark and might need to find a place to spend the night. She was happy to know they were so close.

But the path seemed to run for miles, and the farther along they went, the darker and gloomier the scenery became. Jo found herself missing the large grassy fields that surrounded the houses in Concord, and she had to swallow hard to keep homesickness from overwhelming her.

"Here it is, miss," the liveryman said, and Jo saw in the far distance a huge stone building, more a castle than a house.

"Christopher Columbus!" she whispered.

The liveryman nodded. "Christopher Columbus indeed," he said.

Even with the castle in sight, it took half an hour for the carriage to reach the front doorway. No matter how imposing the Dodge house was, Jo was relieved when they finally arrived, and she gladly accepted help down from the carriage. It felt good to put her feet on solid ground.

The liveryman unloaded Jo's bags and knocked on the heavy wooden door. An aged butler opened it.

"Hello," Jo said, trying to sound confident. "I'm Jo March. That is to say, I'm Pauline's friend Jo. Pauline is staying here with her grandfather, Mr. Dodge."

The butler stared at Jo as though he had never seen a ten-year-old girl before. "Come this way," he finally said.

Jo followed him into the foyer. It was well lit with candles, but even so, it seemed dark and gloomy. She told herself it would look far different in the morning, with the sun pouring in. But she noticed that the windows were small and high up, and the larger ones were made of stained glass. They would look beautiful in the daylight, she was sure, but they probably wouldn't brighten things up much.

"Jo! Jo!"

Jo turned and found Pauline waving merrily to her from the parlor. She broke away from the butler and raced to her friend.

"Oh, it's so good to see you," Jo said. "Pauline, you look wonderful."

"I'm so happy you're here," Pauline said. "I worried all day long that you would change your mind and not visit after all."

"Why would I do that?" asked Jo, although half a dozen reasons raced into her mind.

"Because this place is so horrid," Pauline replied. "Cold and dreary." She touched Jo gently and whispered in her ear. "Exactly the same as Grandfather Dodge."

Jo didn't know what to say. She simply hugged Pauline.

"Where is Mr. Dodge?" Jo asked. "I suppose I should greet him and let him know I've arrived."

"He's in the east wing." Pauline took Jo's hand. "He retires there after supper every day."

"And what do you do?" Jo asked. Pauline led her to a chair that proved to be as uncomfortable as it looked. Still, Jo was pleased to see how well Pauline got around by using a cane. When the girls had met, Pauline had been unable to do anything on her own.

Pauline sat down in a chair by Jo's side. "I read," she said. "Thanks to you, I'm at Perkins, where they've taught me to read Braille. But I must say, it gets boring doing nothing but reading day and night."

"That's why I'm here," Jo said. "Tomorrow we'll take a walk through the gardens."

"There are no gardens," Pauline said. "Grandfather Dodge doesn't believe in them."

"Not even to grow vegetables?" Jo asked. She couldn't imagine a household that didn't grow its own vegetables.

"Oh, there's a vegetable garden," Pauline said. "And there are apple orchards. But there are no flowers. I love flowers, even if I can't see them. I love their scent and the way their petals feel against my skin. Grandfather doesn't like flowers. He doesn't like anything that gives pleasure."

"He can't possibly be so bad," Jo said. "Even Aunt March loves flowers."

"Mrs. March is a circus compared to Grandfather," Pauline said so gloomily that Jo burst out laughing. It took Pauline a moment, but then she laughed also. "I'm glad you decided to come, Jo. You can see the humor in anything, even in this cold, miserable castle."

"It does look like a castle," Jo said.

"It really is one," Pauline told her. "Grandfather had it brought over from Europe stone by stone and reassembled here."

"Why?" Jo asked. "Surely Americans build houses as fine as Europeans do."

"Houses, perhaps, but not castles," Pauline said. "Grandfather Dodge's money is new, you know." She said it as though it were a great scandal, which Jo realized Aunt March would think it was. In Aunt March's eyes, new money was almost worse than no money at all. "Grandfather felt Mother's chances of making a good match would be improved if she lived in a castle," Pauline added.

"Oh, dear," Jo said. "If it takes a castle, then Meg and Beth and Amy and I are certainly doomed."

"I think Mother married Father to escape from here," Pauline said. "Her own mother died when she was eight. She never comes to visit. I've hardly ever been here myself. Even on the hottest days it's cold, and it never feels dry. I know everything is dark to me, but somehow things are even darker here. Oh, Jo, I hate it, and Grandfather Dodge does nothing to make me like it any the more."

"Then I shall," said Jo. "It's exciting to be in a castle. I've never been in one before, and I think it was grand of Mr. Dodge to go to the bother of putting one here. Trust me, Pauline. Now that I've arrived, this castle will be fun again."

But even as she uttered her declaration, Jo had doubts. It was hard to believe this castle had ever seen happy times.

CHAPTER 3

*A*unt March had a half dozen servants, so Jo was accustomed to seeing maids and butlers about a house, but it still took her aback to find one unpacking her meager possessions in the room where she'd be sleeping. Pauline might not be able to see the patches on her dresses, and Jo was coming to believe that Mr. Dodge wouldn't bother to notice them, but the maid would see everything and know just what it meant.

"I can take care of my own things," Jo said. "That is to say, thank you, but truly, I can take care of myself."

"Whatever you say, miss," the maid replied.

"Don't mind her, Mabel," Pauline said. "Jo is simply unused to servants."

"Very well, Miss Pauline," Mabel replied. "Shall I continue to unpack her belongings?"

"No, that's all right, Mabel," Pauline said. "Thank you again."

Jo felt a wave of anger sweep over her. She hadn't liked Pauline when they first met, and she suddenly remembered why. "Did you have to speak to her that way?" she asked Pauline once Mabel had left the room. "As though I were some kind of dithering idiot?"

"Yes," Pauline said. "Jo, I'm sorry, but Grandfather can't keep any of his servants. I've been here only two weeks, and already two maidservants and one footman have left."

"Why?" Jo asked. "Is Mr. Dodge that difficult?"

"He's only part of the problem," Pauline replied. "I'm not supposed to know this, but I overheard Mabel talking to Mrs. Haywood, the cook, and she said she wasn't going to stay here any longer than she had to, because this house was so horrible."

"It's just a castle," Jo said. "I'd think it would be exciting to work in a castle." She thought about all the plays she'd written, all set in castles, and realized she was eager to explore. Her plays would be ever so much better if she knew what a castle was truly like.

"It's not just a castle," Pauline said, lowering her voice. "I know I shouldn't be eavesdropping, but it's been so boring here, Jo, that I've taken to listening to any bit of conversation I can. Mrs. Haywood told Mabel that Grandfather Dodge could never keep servants because everyone believes the castle is haunted."

"Haunted?" Jo asked. "Really?"

Pauline nodded. "Grandfather Dodge put this castle up thirty years ago," she said, "when Mother was our age. And while Mother has never spoken to me of it, one of my sisters told me that Mother said she always thought this house was haunted by ghosts who resented having their home transported all the way to the United States."

"Sisters always say such things," Jo said. "You should hear some of what I've said to Amy."

"But the servants think it is true, and so do the tradesmen," Pauline declared. "I'm beginning to as well."

"Are you really?" Jo asked, nestling on her bed. It felt cold and clammy, but Jo suspected she'd have no trouble falling asleep that night, ghosts or no ghosts.

"I feel things," said Pauline. "Sometimes, Jo, I feel things no one else can, perhaps because of my blindness. Take Grandfather, for example. I don't believe that man has ever smiled."

"But you couldn't see him smile even if he did," Jo pointed out.

"That's just what I mean," Pauline said. "If he did smile at me, I would sense it. I never have. But I have sensed cold things in this house, things that just aren't what they should be. Oh, I can't explain it. I just know something isn't right."

"All the better," Jo said. "You know, Pauline, Amy thought I'd meet dukes and princes here. But I think it will be far more entertaining to meet even one ghost instead!"

CHAPTER 4

J o was uncertain how frightening it might be to encounter a ghost, but she suspected it could be no worse than meeting Mr. Dodge for the first time.

When she saw him the next day at the noontime meal, she wondered whether he was still alive. Never before had she seen such a thin man. Mr. Dodge was old, gray, and so slender that Jo could almost see his bones beneath his clothing. She glanced over at Pauline and marveled that such a lively girl could be related in any way to this walking corpse of a man.

"Grandfather, this is my friend Jo March,"

Pauline said. "Jo, this is my grandfather, Mr. Dodge."

"It's a pleasure to meet you," Jo said, with the prettiest curtsey she could manage.

"Hmpf!" said Mr. Dodge.

Pauline seemed to have nothing more to say. Jo followed her lead and sat down at the table. A bowl filled with wax fruit rested in the center, a fact that startled Jo, as it was summertime and real fruit was so plentiful. She looked at Mr. Dodge, marveling at his resemblance to the wax fruit, and tried hard not to giggle.

"Your friend is smiling," Mr. Dodge said to Pauline.

Jo wondered if that was some sort of crime. "We smile a lot in my family," she said. "There's so much to rejoice in."

Mr. Dodge and Pauline remained silent.

"Gardens, for example," Jo said, hating the silence. "Pauline and I walked through the vegetable gardens this morning. They're very impressive, Mr. Dodge. I didn't even know what some of the vegetables were. I'm sure my father would enjoy a chance to study the plants. He loves to garden, you know."

"How should I know that?" Mr. Dodge asked.

Jo suspected she'd just been insulted, but she was so pleased to have gotten Mr. Dodge to talk, she didn't care. "You're right, of course," she said. "I just always assume everyone knows my father, because he travels so much, and so many fine people respect him and value his friendship."

"The friendship of a gardener?" Mr. Dodge asked.

"Father is a minister," Jo said. "But he respects any man who works hard and is honest and good."

"Are you honest and good?" Mr. Dodge asked as one of the maids served him some mutton.

"I'm honest," Jo said. "Honest enough to admit I'm not always good."

"Jo is good," Pauline said. "Her whole

family is, Grandfather. They're kind and loving and loyal. Any girl would think herself fortunate to be their friend."

Mr. Dodge nodded, although he no longer seemed interested. Pauline too retreated into silence.

Gardens didn't seem to be that successful a topic, Jo decided, but there had to be something they could all talk about. Otherwise there would be thirteen dreadful dinners to look forward to.

"Pauline tells me this castle comes from Europe," Jo said as the maid gave her another serving of carrots.

"From Bavaria," Mr. Dodge replied.

"I think that's perfectly splendid," said Jo. "All the way from Bavaria. Of course, I've never been to Europe, although I hope to someday. I should love to go to Bavaria. Are there still many castles there?"

"I believe so," Mr. Dodge said. "I know I left a few behind."

"Did you have many to choose from?" Jo asked. "My family has moved on occasion, but we've never thought of living in a castle."

"I had my fair share," Mr. Dodge replied. "If your family is still interested, there are a few castles I could recommend."

Jo wasn't sure if Mr. Dodge was teasing her. "We can't afford a castle," she said. "But I look forward to exploring this one so that I can tell my parents and sisters all about it."

"Is it all right for us to walk around, Grandfather?" Pauline asked, and Jo suddenly realized why her friend had been so insistent that they spend the morning outside. Pauline clearly believed she needed her grandfather's permission to wander through the interior of the castle.

"Don't break anything," was Mr. Dodge's sole response.

"We won't, I promise," Jo said. "Pauline, what fun it will be to see all this castle has to offer."

Pauline looked doubtful, but Jo knew she was right. A genuine castle would have many wonderful secrets to reveal.

The rest of the meal was eaten in silence, in spite of Jo's efforts to engage Mr. Dodge in conversation. It made Jo appreciate all the more the animated meals with her family. They always had something to discuss. Even mealtime with Aunt March present, and prone to lecturing, was more enjoyable than this. Jo ate quickly, eager for the meal to end so that she and Pauline could explore the castle.

Eventually Mr. Dodge excused himself, and as soon as he did, Jo took Pauline by the arm and insisted they begin their tour.

Pauline led Jo through a maze of halls to what she called the north wing. "Grandfather's rooms are in the east wing," she said. "You and I are in the west wing. The south wing is where the common rooms are, the parlors and dining hall. But nothing is in the north wing."

"Where do the servants sleep?" Jo asked.

"They have rooms in the east wing," Pauline replied. "Grandfather sleeps there because he likes to awaken early each day. The south wing is the warmest; that's why it's used the most. But the north wing is cold and damp and dreary and has no purpose other than to give the castle four sides."

"How many rooms does this castle have?" Jo asked. It felt as though the girls had been walking for miles, and they'd yet to reach the north wing.

"Fifty or sixty—I don't know for sure," Pauline said. "I cannot understand why Grandfather continues to live here. Make this next right turn, Jo, and we should be there."

Jo followed Pauline and entered a long narrow room. "Christopher Columbus!" she said. "There's armor here, the sort knights used to wear."

"It came with the castle," Pauline explained. "Grandfather bought it with all its furnishings."

"And its ghosts," Jo said. For the first time she could believe something unearthly lived in the castle. For dark as the rest of the house had been, the north wing was even darker, and in spite of the warmth of the day, she felt a chill deep inside her.

"I've never been here," Pauline said. "I wouldn't have the courage now, except you're by my side, Jo."

"It's not that bad," Jo said. "Just dank and dreary." She led Pauline through a curtained doorway—and gasped. A woman was standing deathly still in the middle of the room.

"What is it?" Pauline asked. "What do you see?"

"A ghost," Jo said. "A woman ghost."

"Are you sure?" Pauline asked. "Grandfather keeps his statues in this wing."

Jo moved slowly toward the ghost and discovered to her great embarrassment that the apparition was indeed nothing more than a statue. "You're right," she admitted. "It's merely a figure in marble. But from a distance she looked like a ghost."

"What does a ghost look like?" Pauline asked.

Jo thought about all the ghost stories she'd ever read. "You can see through them," she said. "Which, of course, you can't with a statue. Sometimes they have blood dripping from their eyes or their mouths or their hearts, depending on whether they were stabbed or not. There was once a headless horseman, so a ghost can be that way too. They really are dreadful creatures."

"Then why are you so eager to see one?" Pauline asked. "Wouldn't it be better just to leave a ghost alone?"

"For most people," Jo said. "But I write about such things, and I owe it to my art to look for ghosts wherever I might find them."

"Then I suppose I'll look along with you," Pauline said.

"I'm glad," Jo said. "Because in this castle I could get lost looking and turn into a ghost myself!"

"Pauline? Pauline, wake up."

"Hmmm?" Pauline murmured sleepily.

"I just heard the clock strike three," Jo said. "Everyone is asleep except us."

"Except you," Pauline said. "Leave me alone, Jo."

"If you're awake enough to argue, you're awake enough to look for ghosts," Jo said. She gently shook her friend again. "Come on. You promised you'd search with me."

"But it's three o'clock in the morning," Pauline protested. "Surely even ghosts sleep."

"Ghosts love late-night hours," Jo said.

"They do their worst mischief when the world is sleeping."

"Smart ghosts," Pauline muttered, but Jo saw to her satisfaction that Pauline was stretching and slowly moving her body.

It was hard to make out anything in the night, and Jo knew she would need Pauline's skills to wander in the darkness if she was to find her way to the north wing. "I've been thinking in my room since we went to bed," Jo said. "We need a reason to be up so late."

"Haven't you slept at all?" Pauline asked.

"I suppose I must have," Jo said. "But mostly I've been thinking. It's unlikely one of the servants would be up, but just in case, we need a reason to be walking around."

"Jo, they're servants," Pauline said. "They don't care what we do."

"It doesn't matter," Jo said. "I came up with a reason anyway. We'll just say that I was thirsty and decided to go to the kitchen to get some water."

"And why am I coming with you?" Pauline asked.

81

"Because you're thirsty also," said Jo. "Admit it, Pauline. Wouldn't a glass of water taste good right now?"

"I'm more sleepy than thirsty," Pauline replied. "But if you need a reason, I'm sure that's as good as any."

"Excellent," Jo said. "We'll go to the kitchen and get some water, then we'll get lost on our way back and end up in the north wing."

Pauline looked as though she might protest some more, but instead she got her cane and led Jo through the west wing and into the south wing, where the kitchen was.

The house had been frightening in daylight, but it was even more disturbing in the middle of the night. No candles burned to light the way, and even holding on to Pauline, Jo found herself bumping into walls and furnishings.

"Quiet," Pauline whispered after Jo cried, "Ouch!"

"I can't help it," Jo said. "This castle is so

crowded with furniture, there can't possibly be any room for ghosts."

"That would be fine with me," Pauline said. "We should be close to the kitchen now."

"We are," Jo said. There was just enough moonlight shining through the small windows for her to make out a stove ahead. She and Pauline moved a bit faster, until they reached the kitchen. It took some searching to find drinking glasses, but they did, and Jo filled them both from the pump.

"Why don't we just drink our water here?" Pauline asked.

"Because we need the glasses to prove we were here," Jo said. "Take a sip if you're thirsty, and then let's find our way to the north wing."

"I never said I was thirsty," Pauline protested, but she drank half her glass of water anyway. Jo, who found ghost hunting thirst-inducing work, drank so much of her water that she had to refill the glass.

"Can we go now?" Pauline asked. "I'd really

like to sleep some more before we have to get up for breakfast."

"A fine idea," Jo said. "Lead on, Pauline, and we'll soon be in bed."

"Not soon enough," Pauline said, but she took Jo by the hand and steered her toward the castle's north wing.

They had just reached the drafty wing when Jo screamed in terror. Something cold and metallic seemed to have leaped out at her.

"What is it?" Pauline cried. "Jo, are you all right?"

"I think so," Jo said, breaking away from Pauline so that she could rub her right side. "Oh, it was one of those knights in armor," she said. "I was afraid our ghost was armed."

"Don't call him 'our ghost,'" Pauline said. "He's your ghost, or Grandfather's, but he certainly isn't mine. And there may be more than one."

"I can see a bit better here," Jo said. "The moon is full tonight, and it's casting quite a bit of light."

"There's nothing to see, I'm sure," Pauline said. "Come on, Jo. Let's go back to bed now."

"Just a few more rooms," Jo pleaded. She pushed ahead for a bit, only to realize Pauline was no longer by her side.

"Pauline?" she called.

There was no answer.

"Pauline?" she called again.

"Here, Jo. I'm in here." Pauline's voice sounded strange and far away. "Come quickly."

Jo raced to find her friend. She bumped into a statue, and only at the last second was she able to prevent it from crashing onto the floor. "Pauline, call to me," Jo said. "I don't know where you are."

"I'm here, Jo," Pauline said. "Please hurry. There's something wrong, I just know it."

Jo plunged through the rooms, no longer caring what she might bump into. "Keep talking to me, Pauline," she said. "I need to hear your voice."

"I'm scared, Jo," Pauline said. "Really scared."

"Don't worry," Jo said, although her own heart was pounding. "I'm almost there."

"Please, Jo," Pauline cried. "I don't want to be alone."

Jo searched room after empty room. She had no idea if she was moving closer to Pauline or farther away. Then she felt the cold, a different sort of cold from any she'd known before. It was a cold not of winter but of death. She followed its trail, unwillingly but with all her courage, until she could just make out Pauline's figure in the distance.

"I see you!" she cried. "Oh, Pauline!"

"There's something here," Pauline said. "I can feel it. Can you see anything, Jo?"

Jo wasn't sure. In the dim moonlight she thought she saw a shape floating by Pauline's side.

"Just keep calm," Jo said, as much to herself as to Pauline. "I'm here, and I'll take care of things."

"What is it?" Pauline cried. "Oh, Jo, I'm so scared."

Jo inched closer to her friend. Whatever was by Pauline's side was not human, that much Jo knew. But it didn't resemble any of the ghosts Jo had read about. No blood dripped from its face. Indeed, it had no face, no features at all. It looked like a sheet of ice floating in midair, ice so thin that Jo could see right through it.

She shifted her weight to one side to see what the ghost would do. The ghost didn't seem to care. It only moved closer to Pauline.

"Pauline, it's interested in you, not me," Jo said. "Try moving very slowly to your right and let's see what happens."

Pauline took a single step away. The ghost slowly moved alongside her.

"It's colder now," Pauline asked. "Jo, are you still here?"

"I am, and so is the ghost," Jo said. "It doesn't seem to want to leave you."

"I feel it getting stronger," Pauline said, her voice quavering with fear. "Jo, what should I do?"

"Try walking away calmly," Jo said. "Act as though you're unaware of it."

"I'll try," Pauline said.

Jo remembered how brave Pauline could be. "Just take one step," she said. "Then another and another, as though you've gotten your glass of water and we're heading back to bed."

Pauline did as Jo suggested, but the ghost moved along with her.

"Jo, that's not working," Pauline said. "It's only getting stronger."

"Stand still, then," Jo said. "I need to think."

Pauline stood motionless, almost turning into one of those lifeless statues that had frightened Jo so.

Pauline began to cry. "Jo, I can feel the ghost all over me. It's trying to take over my body. Please hurry and do something before it gains control."

Jo looked at Pauline, and indeed the ice creature had enveloped her friend. Little icicles were forming on Pauline's hair.

"Do something," Pauline said, her voice getting weaker. "Save me. . . ."

Jo didn't know what to do. She searched for

a weapon but couldn't find one. The only thing she had was the glass of water in her hands. Without thinking, she flung the water at the ghost, not caring if she drenched Pauline in the process.

There was a blinding blast of light, followed by an unearthly shriek. "Pauline!" Jo screamed. "Pauline!"

Then there was no sound at all. The silence was even more frightening than the noise had been. As Jo regained her ability to see in the near darkness, she heard Pauline's voice, gaining in strength.

"Jo," Pauline said. "Jo, are you there?"

"I'm right here." Jo rushed to her friend's side. "Pauline, can you feel me?"

"Oh, yes," Pauline said. "It's gone, I can tell. It's gone." She collapsed onto the floor, and Jo sat down with her. The girls held on to each other for a moment, before they began half laughing and half crying from relief.

"And what is this?"

Jo screamed at the sound.

"Grandfather?" Pauline asked.

"Who else might it be?" Mr. Dodge asked.

Pauline squeezed Jo's hand. "What are you doing here?" she asked.

"I might ask the same of you," he said. "I heard shouts and screams and all sorts of peculiar noises and thought I should investigate. What's been going on?"

For once in her life Jo didn't know what to say. In some ways Mr. Dodge was more frightening than even the ghost had been.

"Pauline, I'm waiting for an explanation," Mr. Dodge said.

Pauline sat up and straightened out her nightgown. "I'm sorry, Grandfather," she said. "But I didn't see a thing."

For a moment there was total silence. Then Mr. Dodge smiled.

Jo smiled also, hoping Pauline could sense the tension lifting. But Pauline didn't need to, because in a moment Mr. Dodge was laughing out loud. And as Jo and Pauline joined in his laughter, Jo felt the ghost's coldness replaced by the warmth of joy and life.

"Come, girls," Mr. Dodge said. "I think you've had enough adventures for one night."

"I think so too, Grandfather," Pauline said. "Whenever I'm with Jo, there's always an adventure."

"We'll see what tomorrow brings us, then," Mr. Dodge said. "Won't we, Pauline?"

"We certainly will, Grandfather," Pauline said. She put her small hand in her grandfather's, and Jo smiled again. It had taken a ghost to make Pauline and Mr. Dodge aware of each other's love. With such a happy ending, though, Jo didn't mind her ghostly scare. For now the castle was filled with happiness, which Jo knew would last long after she returned to her own loving home.

Beth's Ghostly Tale

CHAPTER 1

$f$or as long as Beth could remember, Aunt March had scared her.

Of course, most people scared Beth. Strangers always did. But she was happy and comfortable with her parents; her sisters, Meg, Jo, and Amy; the family housekeeper, Hannah; and most other people she'd known all her life. The only exception was Aunt March.

For some reason Aunt March frightened Beth. She could never do anything right in Aunt March's eyes. Even Jo, with her wild and noisy ways that gave Aunt March headaches, was preferred over Beth.

Beth didn't mind that Aunt March didn't

care for her. She didn't care for Aunt March and was just as happy not to have to visit or make conversation with her. But Aunt March was a woman who believed in obligations, and it seemed one of her obligations was to spend time occasionally with Beth.

This time at least Beth wouldn't be paying a call on Aunt March alone. Amy was going with her, and Beth knew how much Aunt March enjoyed Amy's company.

"Do keep her busy," Beth begged Amy as the two girls approached the mansion that was Aunt March's home.

"I always keep her busy," Amy replied. "I like Aunt March."

Beth sighed. Amy was her younger sister and a dear one, but she could never understand why Amy enjoyed Aunt March so, unless it was because Aunt March babied and spoiled her.

Aunt March's butler let them in, instructing them to wait for their hostess in the front parlor. Beth told herself she should be glad of the wait, since it meant less time for the visit, but knowing Aunt March was about to appear only made her more anxious.

"Honestly, Beth," Amy said, carefully picking up one of the many knickknacks that decorated the parlor. "You'd think you were on the way to the gallows."

Beth noticed a china figurine of a kitten. She would have loved to pick it up and examine it, but she knew if she did, Aunt March would walk in. And Beth was certain she'd break the figurine at that precise moment. Either she'd drop it or perhaps she'd crush it with her bare hands, but breakage was guaranteed.

So Beth just stood and looked and worried until finally Aunt March arrived.

And when she did, she was dusty. Beth was startled, since Aunt March was always impeccably groomed.

"I have been in the attic," Aunt March declared, "looking for something that should have been easily found." She stared at Beth, who started to feel it was all her fault.

"What were you looking for, Aunt March?" Amy asked.

"A pair of scissors," Aunt March replied. "There are some bolts of cloth up there, and I cut a piece of material earlier to take to my seamstress. I must have forgotten to bring the scissors down, however. When I went back to look for them just now, they weren't to be found. Very annoying."

"I could go and look for them," Beth said softly.

"Speak up, child," Aunt March said. "I can never hear a word you say. Your sisters all speak clearly, and Jo positively bellows, but you whisper. It's a wonder anyone can hear you."

Beth cleared her throat. "I said I could look for the scissors," she said. "In your attic, I mean. If you want me to."

"I should be very pleased to have you look," Aunt March said. "Amy, would you object to your sister's leaving us for a few minutes?"

"Not at all. I'd enjoy having time to visit with you on my own, Aunt March," Amy said. Amy always knew the proper thing to say, while Beth could hardly choke out an offer of help.

98

"Very well," Aunt March said. "See if you can find those missing scissors, Beth. I shall be most grateful to you if you can."

It took all Beth's willpower not to run out of the parlor. "I'll look very hard for them, Aunt March," she said, no longer caring if her great-aunt could hear her. She had a reason to leave the parlor, and that was good enough for her.

CHAPTER 2

*A*unt March's attic was enormous, almost the size of Beth's family's home, but nowhere near as comfortable or inviting. Beth had never been up here before. She hardly went into her own family's attic, since that was Jo's private place, where Jo wrote her many plays.

As Beth looked around she decided that Aunt March's attic was not unlike Aunt March. Everything was in place. There were many, many crates, each one carefully labeled. One crate held china, another bolts of material, another old clothes, and yet another paintings and statuary. Beth enjoyed her tour. There was enough to furnish an entire household.

Beth's own family had no such riches. Still, they had all they needed, and while Beth would have liked a new and better piano, she would not have traded a single thing for all Aunt March's wealth.

Beth was in no hurry to return to the parlor, so she took her time looking around, trying to find the scissors. It felt wonderful to be alone in Aunt March's house, not having to worry about what to say next and how loudly to say it. As it happened, Beth found the scissors fairly soon, but she decided Aunt March would have no way of knowing that. So she started to look at several of the packed-up treasures.

As she walked to a far corner she was surprised to discover a treasure that was neither packed nor wrapped in cloth. It was a painting of a young woman, hardly more than a girl, really, dressed in old-fashioned attire.

Beth stared at the painting. The girl had blue eyes and light brown hair pinned high. Her dress was ivory with a light blue sash that matched her eyes. She was holding a basket of flowers in the crook of her arm, and her right hand held a red rose.

Beth had never seen such a beautiful painting before. She loved the way the girl looked, so solemn, yet with life in her eyes. Beth knew this was a girl who loved flowers, who loved life, and who was loved in turn by those who knew her.

Beth looked more closely at the painting. In the girl's left hand was a handkerchief. It wasn't easy to make out, but Beth thought the handkerchief was embroidered with the initials *E.M.*

"E.M.," she whispered to herself. Those were her own initials, for Elizabeth March. True, no one called her Elizabeth. But that was her given name. She wondered if the girl in the picture bore the same name. Not that E.M. looked anything like Beth. She was older than ten, for one thing, and prettier, and Beth had the sense that although the girl wasn't smiling, she wanted to be. Her eyes seemed filled with

laughter, the way Jo's sometimes got when she knew a joke before anyone else did.

In a funny way, Beth thought, she felt as close to the girl in the painting as she did to anybody she knew, except of course for her sisters. Perhaps E.M. was some sort of relative. Beth didn't know enough about clothing to be able to date the painting that way, but she was sure it was old, and she knew it was wonderful.

"Beth! Beth!"

Amy was calling her. Beth could hear her sister's footsteps on the floor below. In the blink of an eye Beth made some decisions. She knew she didn't want to share E.M. with anybody, not even Amy. She also knew she wanted to see more of E.M. She wanted a chance to memorize the painting, to visit it the way one would visit a dear friend. For Beth felt E.M. was a friend, and one she longed to know better.

"I'm coming, Amy," Beth cried in a voice so loud that Aunt March could probably hear her two stories down in the front parlor.

"Don't forget the scissors," Amy called back.

Beth laughed. She had put the scissors down

when she first spotted the painting. Now, in her rush to prevent Amy from coming up the attic stairs, she had completely forgotten about them. Quickly she grabbed them.

"Really, Amy," Beth said as she made her way down the stairs, scissors carefully in hand. "What sort of goose do you take me for, thinking I'd forget what I was sent for?"

"A happy goose?" Amy replied. "You look very happy, Beth. Whatever did you find in that attic?"

"Nothing," Beth said. "Nothing at all." And she smiled at the secret she felt she shared with her new friend, E.M.

CHAPTER 3

$\mathcal{B}$eth thought about making up reasons why she needed to visit Aunt March, but she hated to lie. Still, she had to see more of E.M., and she didn't feel she could explain why. Not even to Jo, her favorite sister, or to Marmee.

There was a special bond between E.M. and herself, and she felt that if she told anyone, the magic would be broken.

So Beth simply decided to pay regular calls on Aunt March, timing them as best she could for when the old woman would be napping or paying calls of her own, or even when she had other company.

"That's all right," Beth would say to the butler as he informed her of Aunt March's current activities. "I shan't bother her. I'll just go up to the attic and entertain myself."

Beth wasn't at all sure whether the butler was telling Aunt March of her visits or keeping them to himself. Perhaps he thought the March girls were all a little mad, and Beth the maddest of all.

Beth didn't care. Aunt March's butler no longer frightened her. Aunt March hardly did herself. Nothing really mattered except going to the attic, finding the painting, and staring into E.M.'s blue eyes.

Beth grew to know every detail of the painting by heart. E.M. stood by a table on which there was a vase filled with roses. The girl wore a good locket that bore the same initials as the handkerchief. Beth, who wasn't one for possessions, would have loved to own such a locket. She noted that E.M.'s cheeks were pink and her fingers long and delicate. Beth wondered if she played the piano. She wondered who had given her the locket, who had embroidered the handkerchief. But more than anything Beth wanted to know what had become of E.M.

Beth supposed she could ask Father or Aunt March about a girl in the family, perhaps named Elizabeth, but she sensed the time wasn't right. She wasn't ready yet to let anyone else know how much she loved the painting in the attic.

Still, she was very curious, and she decided that Jo might know a way to find out. Beth practiced her questions until she was comfortable enough to ask.

The mission was so important to Beth that she even went up to the Marches' attic, where Jo was sitting at her desk, working on her latest play, *The Secrets of the Duchess*. Beth knew how Jo hated to be interrupted, but she didn't want to question her where others might hear and start asking questions of their own.

"May I come in?" she asked, even though she already was in.

Jo turned, and Beth saw her ink-stained face and hands, along with a look of irritation.

"What do you want?" Jo asked in a tone Beth was unaccustomed to hearing.

"I'm sorry," Beth said. "I know I'm bothering you."

"No, I'm the one who's sorry," said Jo in a softer voice. "You would never come unless it was important. Sit down, Bethy, and tell me what's on your mind."

"It's really not important," Beth said. "Not to anyone but me, I suppose."

"Then it is important," Jo said. "You never ask a thing of any of us, and here I go snapping just because you interrupted act three."

"Is it a good act?" Beth asked.

Jo smiled. "Not as good as I'd like it to be," she said. "Talk to me, Bethy, and freshen my thoughts."

"I was just wondering how someone could learn more about their family," Beth said.

"Do you mean this family?" Jo asked with a laugh. "Our house is too small for secrets. What do you think you want to know?"

"I don't mean I want to know about our

109

parents or sisters," Beth said. "I mean our ancestors."

"You could ask Father and Marmee," Jo said. "They love to talk about their families. And if you get Aunt March on the subject, she'll never stop talking. Try it sometime. Her stories are actually rather interesting."

Beth swallowed. "Suppose I wanted to learn something about—oh, I don't know—say, the Marches, but without asking anyone. Father's so busy, and Aunt March frightens me, and Marmee loves the Marches but they're not her family. How could I find something out?"

"You could read old family letters," Jo said. "Or documents. Or even look at the family Bible. It has a family tree in it listing our ancestors. Except it belongs to Aunt March, so you'd have to ask her permission."

Beth shuddered at the thought. "No."

"All right, then," Jo said. "Go to the cemetery. We have many March ancestors buried there, with names and dates. You'll find Uncle

March, for one, and Father's parents and grandparents, and lots of other Marches I hardly know about."

"That's a splendid idea," Beth said. "I'll go over right now."

"Do you want me to come with you?" Jo asked. "The duchess can keep her secrets awhile longer."

"Thanks," Beth said. "But I think I'd rather look on my own."

"Won't the graveyard frighten you?" Jo asked.

"Why should it?" Beth replied. "I'll be home well before dark. Thank you, Jo. It was a wonderful idea." Beth ran out of the attic before Jo had a chance to ask any more questions.

It was a cool April day, and she put on her shawl before walking to the cemetery. Beth had been there once, for Uncle March's funeral, and had little trouble finding the March family plot.

Quite a few Marches were buried there, and Beth didn't know whom she might be looking for. There was an Elihu March, who certainly wasn't Beth's E.M., and an Ellen Baker March, but Beth didn't think she was E.M. either, since Beth was sure E.M. had been born a March and hadn't married into the family.

Beth continued to look, noting all the fine old March names. There were William March and Mary March, a handful of babies who had died before they could be named, James March and Abigail Hendrick March, young Marches and old Marches, Marches who had been born before the Revolution and two Marches, Benjamin and John, who had died during it.

Beth paused for a moment at her grandparents' grave and again at Uncle March's. She thought about them and the fine long lives they'd lived. She thought about E.M., wondering where she was buried or if perhaps she was still alive. She thought about herself. Would she be buried in the same graveyard as all these other Marches? What did her life have in store for her? Would she have children and grandchildren who would someday visit her in the cemetery?

Beth shivered. The sun was setting, and the day was losing its warmth. E.M.'s secrets would have to remain hidden a little while longer.

C H A P T E R   4

The next morning Beth woke up with a cold. She ran a fever for a few days, and everyone made a fuss over her. They brought her hot soup to drink, her dollies to tend to, and the kittens to enjoy.

It wasn't so bad in the daytime, when her sisters were home and spent all their free time with her. But at night Beth dreamed of E.M. She was certain the girl in the portrait was trying to tell her something, but Beth could never quite hear her.

It was a week before Beth was strong enough to get out of bed, and it took a few days more before she could persuade Marmee that she was well enough to pay a call on Aunt March.

"I've never known you to be so eager to see her," Marmee said as Beth pleaded with her to be allowed to go.

"I won't stay long, I promise," Beth said.

"I'm not even sure Aunt March will be in," Marmee said. "I believe she mentioned she was going to Boston for a few days."

Beth could hardly believe her luck. "If she isn't in, I'll just stroll for a bit," she said. "I've been inside for so long, Marmee. I want to see the trees budding and the flowers blossoming."

Marmee laughed. "Enjoy yourself," she said. "Just don't overdo and catch another cold."

"I'll be fine," Beth said. She felt so much better that she ran most of the way to Aunt March's. To her delight, the butler informed her that indeed Aunt March was away for a few days.

"I need to go to the attic to look for something," Beth said. "I left it behind when I visited last, and it's been bothering me ever since."

The butler ushered her in, and Beth scurried

up to the attic. There, right where she had left it, was the painting.

"I'm back," Beth whispered. "Have you missed me?"

"Yes, I have."

Beth turned around, startled by the voice. It belonged to a girl who was standing in a dark corner of the attic.

"It's you," Beth said. "E.M."

The girl nodded. "I've been wondering when you'd come back," she said. "I've come to enjoy your visits so much. It gets lonely up here."

"But how did you get out of the painting?" Beth asked.

"I'm not sure," the girl replied. "I've tried and tried for ever so long, and today I was finally able to. I was so sure you were coming, and here you are."

"I've been ill," Beth said. "I've had a cold. But I knew you wanted to tell me something."

"I do," the girl said. "I need your help, and I don't even know where to begin."

"Why don't we start with our names?" Beth said. "I've been calling you by your initials,

116

E.M., but I'm sure you have more of a name than that."

The girl laughed. Beth had never heard such a happy sound before. "I'm Elizabeth March," she said. "But all who love me call me Eliza."

"I was sure of it," Beth said. "I'm Elizabeth March also, but everyone calls me Beth."

Eliza seemed to float toward her. "It's a joy to meet you at last," Eliza said. "Of course, after all these years stuck in a painting, it would be a joy to meet most anybody."

"How long has it been, exactly?" Beth asked.

"I can't be certain," replied Eliza. "What year is it now?"

"Eighteen fifty-eight," Beth said.

"Oh, my," Eliza said. "My portrait was painted in 1758, although I lived for two years after that."

"Then you're dead," Beth said. "I was afraid you were, but I couldn't find you in the March family plot."

"Oh, I wouldn't be there," Eliza said. "But

118

my father is. William March. Perhaps you've seen his tombstone?"

"I have!" Beth said. "I visited the cemetery about ten days ago. There was no mention of you on his tombstone. I read them all, looking for your name."

Eliza nodded sadly. "I was the world to him," she said. "Especially after my mother died. I loved him dearly too, but I was young and full of life and would not listen to reason."

"What did you do?"

"I broke his heart," Eliza said. "I ran off with a British soldier. Trevor looked dashing in his uniform, and I thought I loved him. He swore he loved me. Then I found myself with child, and I never saw or heard from him again. Father would have nothing to do with me. I wrote to him, but he never responded. Finally, when I could go on no longer, I went back to his house to beg his forgiveness, only to be told he had died the night before, his heart broken by my treachery."

"And then you died too," Beth said.

Eliza nodded. "In childbirth. Alone, unloved, and unwanted. The babe died also, and we were buried together in a pauper's grave."

"I'm so sorry," Beth said. "I had so hoped you were happy."

"Oh, I was for a while," Eliza said. "I was headstrong and foolish and used to having my way. I thought I would never know sorrow, until sorrow became my daily bread."

"Have you spoken to anyone since?" Beth asked.

Eliza shook her head. As Beth looked more closely at her, she could see that Eliza no longer was flesh and blood but appeared more two-dimensional, as though indeed she had stepped out of a painting.

"I've spent all these years standing still, wishing my father still loved me," Eliza said.

"I'm sure he never stopped loving you," Beth said. "He was angry. My sister Jo gets angry all the time, but she always loves us."

"I hope you're right," Eliza said. "I've been thinking and thinking all the time you were gone that if I could only let my father know how much I loved him, perhaps he would love me again."

"There must be a way," Beth said.

"That's why I need you," declared Eliza. "It took all my strength, strength born of desperation, to will myself out of this painting. I know somewhere in this attic is the locket Father gave me. Do you see it in the portrait?"

"Of course," Beth said. "But it's not on you now."

Eliza shook her head. "It's in a trunk, I'm certain of it. I sent it back to Father with the last of my letters, but by the time he got it he was too ill to open the envelope. Beth, can you find the locket for me?"

"Do you know which trunk?" Beth asked.

"It's in this corner," Eliza said. "That's why I was there. But my arms have no strength; my fingers cannot bend. Beth, you must find it, and when you do, take it to my father and put it on his grave. He'll know then that I loved him all along, and perhaps he'll forgive me."

"I'll do what I can," Beth promised. She

121

walked over to the corner. Hidden beneath one of the eaves was an old dust-covered trunk with the initials *W.M.* stamped on it.

Ordinarily Beth would have been too frightened to open anything that Aunt March might have regarded as her own. But Eliza's need was so great that Beth didn't care what the consequences might be.

The trunk had once been locked, but it opened almost at Beth's touch. Inside were clothes, books, and a variety of envelopes.

Eliza floated over to Beth's side. "Those envelopes are mine," she said. "My unopened letters to my father."

"He kept them all," Beth said. "That must mean something."

"Perhaps he thought someday he'd forgive me," Eliza replied. "There, Beth. It's that one. See, the envelope that's thicker than the others. It must have my locket in it."

Beth picked up the envelope gingerly. With her fingers trembling, she opened it. Four pages fell out, and with them the locket.

"That's it!" Eliza cried. "Oh, Beth, take it

now and put it on my father's grave. Tell him of my love for him, and beg him to forgive me."

"I shall," Beth said. "And I'll come back and tell you."

"No." Eliza smiled a small smile that was filled with sorrow. "No, Beth. Do what I ask you and then return home. I'll need to be alone. Forgive me, but I know somehow that if I'm to know what is in my father's heart, I must be alone."

Beth nodded. "I'll do what you ask," she said. "Eliza, I just know your father will forgive you. All will be right again."

"If that is true, it will be because of your goodness, not mine," Eliza said. "Now go, and know, Elizabeth March, that you will always be in my heart."

"And you in mine," Beth said. She grasped the locket and took one last look at Eliza before making her way out of the house.

The sun shone on Beth as she raced to the graveyard. She was glad she'd been there just ten days before, since she knew where the graves were, knew just where William March rested.

Beth took a moment to read the tombstone. William L. March was buried next to his wife, Anne Howell March. Their dates of birth and death were listed. Anne Howell March had as her epitaph Loving Wife and Mother. William March's tombstone had no such words. Instead someone had engraved May He Now Rest in Peace.

"I hope you will," Beth whispered to him as

MARCH

William L.

May he now rest in

PEACE

18_d——18_12

she laid the golden locket by the tombstone. "Eliza did love you, and she knew she had done wrong. She begs your forgiveness. Please give it to her, and then she'll know peace as well."

Beth heard the sorrowful cooing of a mourning dove. She wondered if the dove was crying to William, telling him to forgive his daughter and show his love for her again.

Thinking of Eliza, trapped all those years in a painting in an attic, waiting for someone to love her enough to hear her sorrow, Beth whispered, "William, forgive her. Eliza, know peace."

Beth wanted to go back to the attic, yearned to tell Eliza that she had done her bidding, wanted to tell her of the mourning dove and assure her that her father knew her sorrow and that all would be well again. But she chose to respect Eliza's wishes and slowly walked home instead.

Beth knew she couldn't go back to Aunt March's while her great-aunt was away in Boston. It seemed to take forever before the elderly woman returned, but when she did, Beth insisted that she and her mother pay a call.

Aunt March was sitting in the front parlor and seemed pleased enough to see them. Beth forced herself to converse, but all she wanted was to be excused and go to the attic.

Eventually Aunt March and Marmee settled in for a conversation, mostly about whom Aunt March had seen in Boston and where she had shopped. Beth seized the opportunity and went up to the attic.

She headed immediately for the portrait, wondering if Eliza would be able to emerge from it again or if she'd still be wearing the locket.

But the painting wasn't in its usual corner. In fact, it was nowhere in sight.

Thinking it might have been moved, Beth searched behind every crate and in every nook and cranny, but no painting turned up.

Weary, Beth went over to William March's trunk and opened it carefully. Everything was just as she'd left it; the four sheets of Eliza's last letter to her father rested on top of the envelope. Beth picked up the letter and began to read.

Parts of the letter were smudged with streaks, which Beth knew meant Eliza must have cried as she'd written to beg her father's forgiveness. Beth cried also as she reached the end of the letter.

Father, as proof of my love for you, I am returning the locket you so lovingly gave to me. I walked past a pawnbroker's this morning and thought of giving him the locket in exchange for the few pence that would buy me bread. I have not eaten in two days, Father, and I worry for the health of my unborn babe. But I would rather starve than pawn the one thing I still have of you, and I return it to you so that I will never feel the temptation again.

May we meet again on earth, my beloved father, and may you hold your arms out to me and welcome me back to your loving bosom. But know always that I love you and long for your forgiveness.

Beth put the letter back. Surely William would have forgiven Eliza if he'd been well enough to read her plea. Beth could only hope that leaving the locket at his grave had brought peace to them both.

That still didn't explain the missing painting. Beth searched the attic one last time, then went down to the parlor.

"There you are," Aunt March said. "I gather you've been back to my attic."

"Yes, Aunt March."

Aunt March turned to Marmee. "Beth seems to have developed quite a fascination with my dust-filled attic," she said. "She has been paying it all kinds of visits. What, pray tell, has you in its thrall?"

"The painting of Elizabeth March," Beth said. "But I couldn't find it just now. Do you know where it is, Aunt March?"

"A painting?" Aunt March asked.

"The one of the girl holding roses," Beth said. "It's been in the attic every time I've gone up."

"That's not possible," Aunt March said. "I have no such painting."

"Elizabeth March?" Marmee asked, repeating the name. "Beth, what do you know about her?"

"She died in 1760," Beth said. "She was William March's daughter. She ran off with a British soldier, and her father never forgave her."

"That does sound familiar," Aunt March said. "But I know nothing about a painting."

"I do," Marmee said. "Before you were born, Beth, your grandfather told me the story. Elizabeth March was William March's only child. He loved her and spoiled her, and indeed he did have her portrait painted. When she ran off, her father was so angered that he destroyed it."

"Yes, the story is coming back," Aunt March said. "William March was my late husband's great-uncle, and I know there was a scandal involving his daughter. But we certainly never had a painting of her."

"Then there was no painting," Beth said. "It was there only for me."

"What do you mean, child?" Aunt March

looked at Marmee, then back at Beth. "I must say I'm finding you even more difficult to understand than I usually do."

Beth knew she would tell the story someday to Marmee, and for all she knew, Marmee might tell Aunt March. But for now the story was hers, and Eliza's, and William March's. The important thing was that she knew Eliza was free at last, enjoying a freedom that she could know only from her father's love and forgiveness. Beth smiled, feeling Eliza's joy in her very soul.

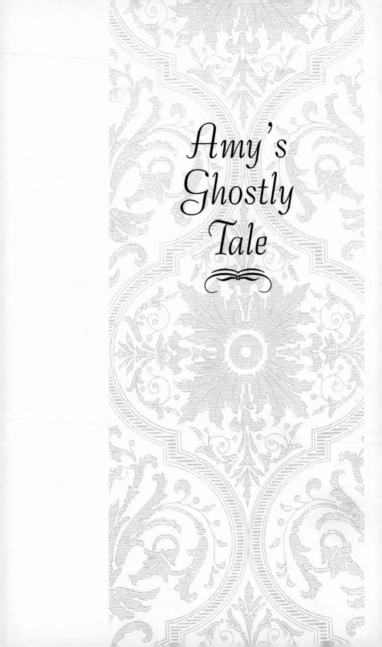

Amy's
Ghostly
Tale

CHAPTER 1

*I*t wasn't fair.

Amy March looked down at her dress and wished, as she'd wished nearly every day of her life, that she had more and better things. More dresses, and better ones. More art supplies, and better ones. The only thing she didn't want more of was older sisters, but on occasion she even wished the ones she had were better. Meg was always willing to accept what came her way, Beth was so shy it was painful to be in school with her, and Jo—well, Jo was the worst. She was rowdy and unladylike, and Amy was always fighting with her.

It was Jo's hand-me-down (by way of Meg

and Beth as well) that Amy was wearing as she stared at Jenny Snow. Jenny had just entered the schoolroom accompanied by her best friend, Susie Perkins.

Jenny and Susie were rich, so Amy knew it was foolish to compare anything of hers to theirs, but she couldn't help it. Sometimes she thought Jenny wore a different dress every single day. And Susie was just as bad. She and Jenny looked as though they'd stepped out of a ladies' magazine, while Amy was always stuck in a dress her three sisters had worn before her.

Someday, Amy told herself, she'd marry a duke or a prince, and she'd be rich and beautiful and own so many dresses that she'd require an entire palace just to hold them. She'd travel abroad every year, going to all the finest museums, where her own paintings would hang. Jenny and Susie would envy her then.

Amy pictured the scene. She was strolling in Paris, her adoring duke by her side, when she spotted Jenny and Susie walking together.

They weren't poor (although it was amusing to picture them selling matches), but no matter how elegant they tried to be, Amy was far better dressed.

"Amy?" they said. "Little Amy March?"

"I'm the Duchess of Paris now," Amy responded. "Come, Duke. The king is expecting us."

Amy's daydream made her smile. It was delicious to imagine herself the envy of girls who treated her with little respect. Amy thought about France. She wasn't sure France had a king anymore, but that didn't matter. A king from some other country could be visiting Paris. Or maybe she and her duke could travel to London, where at least there was a queen. The encounter could even happen in China, for all Amy cared, just as long as she ended up richer than Jenny Snow and Susie Perkins.

"How I wish Father had money," Amy said after school that day. Marmee was out of the house paying calls, so it was safe to express that sentiment to her sisters.

"Money would be nice," Meg agreed. "I should love a new pair of gloves."

"I'd buy new books all the time," Jo said, "instead of having to save my funds to buy just one."

"I'd buy a new piano," Beth said. "Yes, money would be nice."

Amy was pleased that her sisters agreed with her. They rarely did, however, at least not all at the same time. To her dismay, their unanimous sentiment lasted barely a moment. Jo put down the stocking she was darning and shook her head.

"Money isn't everything," she said. "A new piano for Bethy would be nice, but I'm sure many families with grand pianos don't make nearly as nice music as ours does."

"I do enjoy standing around the piano singing every evening," Meg said. "Perhaps if we had money, we wouldn't enjoy ourselves so."

"We couldn't possibly," Jo agreed. "If I had all the books I wanted, I'd probably never read any of them. And Meg, if you had new gloves, we'd never get to see your hands."

Meg stretched her arms out and admired her hands. Amy knew they were Meg's greatest vanity. "Still, a little more money would be nice," Meg said.

"But what if we had to give up something for that money?" Jo persisted. "Surely we'd be forced to make a sacrifice."

"You mean I might have to give up my dollies?" Beth asked. "Just for some money?"

"A fine example," Jo said. "Suppose you were offered a hundred dollars for one of your dolls. Would you take it, Beth?"

Beth shook her head. "I would never sell any of them," she said. "They need me too much."

"Nobody would give Beth a hundred dollars for one of her tattered dolls," Amy said. "That's a foolish example."

"What would you give up, then?" Jo asked. "Would you have Father any other way?"

"Father should never change," Meg said. "And if you mean he might have to give up some of his goodness so that we could have more money, that would never do."

"It doesn't have to be that way," Amy said. "Couldn't Father or Marmee simply be rich? Other people have rich parents. Why couldn't we?"

"Because rich families aren't as happy or good as poor ones," Jo said. "Not that we're poor. Not compared to so many others."

"Jo's right," Meg said. "We should remember those who have so little. There are children in Concord who don't have enough to eat. We never go hungry. We don't wear rags. We're not cold in the winter. We have nothing to complain about."

"I have things to complain about," Amy muttered. "I know Father is good and we have food on our table, but I want pretty dresses and fine art supplies. I want to have every bit as much as Jenny Snow and Susie Perkins."

"Then work to earn it," Jo said. "As I intend to. Otherwise you won't deserve it, and somehow you'll pay for your ill-gotten gains."

"That wouldn't do at all," Beth said. "Try to be patient, Amy, and good."

"Goodness is worth far more than money," Meg said.

"You all make me sick," Amy grumbled. She picked up the sampler she'd been working on and tossed it at them. It had been a terrible day, and Jo had only made it worse, the way she always did. Amy stormed out of the house and slammed the door behind her, as though to shut out her pious sisters and her family's poverty.

CHAPTER 2

*A*my knew she would have to return home, but she was in no hurry. Instead she walked to Walden Pond and sat under a tree. All her sisters occasionally escaped from the house in favor of someplace quiet. Amy usually used her art as an excuse, claiming she wanted to sketch a bird or a tree when all she wanted was peace and privacy.

Today she had no sketchpad or pencils, and she didn't really want her mood to improve. It was all so unfair. Wasn't it bad enough that she didn't have enough money for pretty dresses? Did Jo have to make her sound like a sinner for wanting what they all wanted but only Amy was honest enough to admit?

It was a late spring day, and the sun shone brightly down on the pond. Amy stared at the water, flat as a piece of glass and blue as the sky.

Out of nowhere a breeze arrived, and the once quiet water became choppy. When the trees stopped their dance, Amy noticed a reflection in the pond, a body first, then a face.

Amy looked up to see whose reflection it was. She saw a girl her own age, ten, standing by her side.

And what a girl! Amy thought she'd never seen one so pretty. She had long blond curls, clear blue eyes, and a nose exactly like the one Amy had always wanted. Her dress, too, was just the sort Amy dreamed of owning, a soft blue silk with a white lace collar and cuffs. Around her neck hung a strand of pearls, and on her wrist was a bracelet of rubies and emeralds.

Amy had never seen such an elegantly dressed girl in Concord, and she certainly had never seen one with such beautiful and expensive jewelry. She could only imagine what her sisters would say about a young girl wearing silks and gems, but she didn't care. It was just as she dreamed of herself, with all the things she wanted to wear when she was married to her duke.

"Oh, my," Amy said, nearly speechless.

"May I join you?" the girl asked.

"Please." Amy patted the ground by her side and watched with pleasure as the girl delicately placed her silk parasol, which matched her dress, on the ground. Seemingly out of nowhere, the girl produced a shawl, laid it on the grass, and sat down upon it.

"Are you new to Concord?" Amy asked. "I've never seen you before."

"This is my first time in Concord," the girl said. "All my life I have traveled, and now I am here."

"How fortunate you are," Amy said. "I've never had the chance to go anywhere."

"The world is the same wherever you go," the girl said.

145

"Even Paris?" Amy asked. "Or have you never been to Paris?"

The girl laughed. Her laughter sounded like music, but music far more melodic than any song Beth had ever played on her piano. "I have been everywhere," she said. "There is no real difference between Paris and Concord. Life is unfair no matter where one lives."

"Isn't that the truth," Amy said. "I was just thinking about the very same thing when you came."

The girl nodded. "I sensed your unhappiness," she said. "But I thought you might be willing to speak to me."

"I'm delighted," Amy said. "It's so rare to meet someone as fine as you."

"I can only hope I am as fine as you," the girl said.

Amy smiled. "My name is Amy March."

The girl paused for a moment and looked deep into Amy's eyes. "My name is Amelia," she said. "But I am called Mimi."

"Mimi," Amy repeated. She thought Amelia's nickname was quite elegant. And as she looked in delight at the new girl, she realized that with their blond curls and blue eyes, they actually resembled each other. Perhaps that was why Mimi seemed to like her.

Whatever the reason, Amy was thrilled to have met such a wonderful girl. "I should so like us to be friends," she said.

"We are friends," Mimi replied. "And friends we'll be for as long as you wish, Amy March."

CHAPTER 3

When Amy finally made her way home, she was annoyed to find that no one had missed her. None of her sisters seemed to care that they had angered her so with their lack of understanding.

Any thought of telling them about Mimi, perhaps discussing how they might meet this most delightful girl, but she was too irritated by their lack of concern to share anything with them.

"She's back," was all Jo said as Amy entered the parlor, finding her sisters pretty much as she'd left them.

"Did you have a nice walk?" Meg asked, as though she cared.

"The day is so delightful, we were thinking of all taking a walk," Beth said. "Where did you go, Amy?"

"Out," was all Amy felt like saying.

"Out is a good place to walk," Jo said. "So much sunnier than in."

Meg laughed. Amy grew angry all over again.

"You never take me seriously," she said.

"We treat you the way you deserve to be treated," said Jo. "It's hard to take you seriously when you throw a sampler across a room and stomp your little feet."

"At least my feet are little," Amy said. "They're the feet of a lady, and not a big, headstrong ruffian like you."

Jo only laughed. "You've captured me there all right," she said. "I am a big, headstrong ruffian."

"You are not," Beth said. "You're not that big."

Meg, Jo, and Beth roared with laughter. Amy stared at the other girls and wished she could sacrifice all of them for any amount of money.

"We're sorry, Amy," Meg said. "But you do go on and on about things sometimes."

"I don't care what you think," Amy said, and as soon as she heard the words come out of her mouth, she realized it was true. She didn't care what they thought. She'd known Mimi for only a few minutes, and already Mimi understood her better than her sisters ever had.

Jo put down her darning needle. "Amy, do you care to join us anyway?" she asked. "We truly would enjoy your company as we take our stroll."

"I think not," Amy said. "Take your walk without me."

"I'm sure Amy is tired," Beth said. "She has just been out, after all. That's it, Amy, isn't it? That's why you won't go with us."

"No, that is not it. I simply have no desire to walk with you," Amy said. "Any of you. So go now and leave me be."

"All right," Jo said. "We'll see you later."

"Perhaps you should rest for a bit," Meg said. "We'll all feel better at suppertime."

"I feel well enough now, thank you," Amy said. She stormed out of the parlor and made her way upstairs to her room. At least she'd have it to herself, since Beth would be out walking.

Amy stretched out on her bed, taking care not to wrinkle her dress. Not that it mattered, since it was hardly more than a rag. Life was so unfair.

She closed her eyes and must have fallen asleep, because when she opened them, she was startled to find Mimi perched on the edge of Beth's bed.

"Mimi," Amy said, sitting up suddenly and trying to smooth her dress. "How long have you been here?"

Mimi smiled. "Just a moment. You looked so peaceful, I didn't want to bother you."

"Did anyone see you come in?" Amy asked.

Mimi shook her head. "The house is empty except for you," she replied. "And a servant

151

woman in the kitchen, but she didn't notice me."

"That's Hannah," Amy said, feeling a little guilty that she didn't protest Mimi's description of Hannah, who was far more than a servant woman to the Marches. But it was embarrassing enough to have such a wealthy girl as Mimi see the miserable house Amy lived in. At least Mimi realized they could afford one servant.

Amy wondered how Mimi knew where she lived, but the Marches were well known in town, and she supposed the new girl had asked someone and had been told where to go. "I'm so pleased you've come to visit," she said. "Although I'm sure this home must seem modest to you."

"You deserve better," Mimi said.

"Do you really think so?" Amy asked.

"You know you do," said Mimi. "Someday you'll hardly remember this house or even this town. You'll be like me. You will have lived everywhere and you will be from nowhere."

"I should love to be a great lady," Amy admitted. "Is that foolish of me?"

"It is what you deserve," Mimi said. "You should have diamonds and emeralds, personal maids and castles in Europe. You were born for such riches, Amy, and it is an injustice that you have been deprived of them."

"Yes," Amy said. "Especially when girls like Jenny Snow and Susie Perkins have so much and I have so little."

"Everything they have should be yours," Mimi replied. "You are far more entitled than they are."

Amy wondered how Mimi was aware of what Jenny and Susie had, but she decided Mimi probably knew them. Rich girls always seemed to know other rich girls.

"My sisters are out on a walk," Amy said. "Would you like to stay a bit longer and meet them? You could have supper with us too. I'm sure you're used to much finer, but I know Marmee would love to get to know you."

Mimi gave Amy one of her beautiful smiles.

"I fear I cannot," she said. "I must leave now. I simply wanted to see you again and pledge my friendship."

"Oh, yes," Amy said. "I know we'll be great friends. I've never met anyone as splendid as you, or anyone who understands me so well."

"We will be friends forever," Mimi said. "That is my pledge."

"Mine also," Amy said.

"I will be going, then," Mimi declared. "There is no need to see me out. I will visit you tomorrow if you desire, Amy, and the day after that and the day after that."

"I do desire," Amy said. "Good-bye, Mimi. And thank you for being my friend."

"You have nothing to thank me for," Mimi said, and with the hint of a farewell wave, she floated out of the room and was gone.

CHAPTER 4

Ordinarily Amy liked school, but there were times when she desperately wanted the day to be over, and this day was one of them. Jenny and Susie had showed up in brand-new dresses and ignored Amy all day long. It didn't matter that many other girls wanted to sit with Amy during lunch, or whisper to her while their teacher droned on.

What made Amy feel even worse was that Mimi wasn't at school. She didn't know why she'd been so sure Mimi would be in her class, but she'd wanted it so much that she'd felt sure it would happen. She felt somehow that Mimi had let her down, although she suspected a girl as fine as Mimi was probably taught at home by governesses and tutors.

The school day eventually ended, and Amy scurried out of school, not waiting for Beth, although they usually walked home together. But Amy wasn't sure she wanted to go directly home. True, Mimi knew where she lived, but that didn't mean Mimi would be there waiting for her. A girl like Mimi probably didn't wait for people. She would expect people to wait for her. Amy would have been more than happy to, but she didn't know where to wait.

Still, Amy didn't feel surprised when she spotted Mimi sitting in the town square. She looked even prettier in green than she had in blue.

Mimi smiled as Amy walked over to her. "I was waiting for you," she said.

Amy was thrilled. She almost pointed out that if she'd gone straight home, she would have been nowhere near the town square, but it didn't seem to matter. Mimi would surely have found her. Mimi would have been waiting.

Amy sat down on the bench next to her friend. "I'm so glad to see you," she said. "Jenny and Susie were even worse than usual."

Mimi nodded solemnly. "They are terrible girls," she said.

"I don't know that they're terrible," Amy said. After all, she thought, before she'd met Mimi, Jenny and Susie were the two girls she most wanted to have as friends. "It's just that they have so much more than I do."

"It's wrong that they do," Mimi said flatly. "Look, there they are."

Amy looked over and saw the two girls strolling together. "There's never one without the other," she said. "Jenny thinks the only girl good enough to be her friend is Susie."

"They're fools," Mimi said. "You're better than both of them. Look, Susie has dropped her handkerchief."

"She has," Amy said. "And Jenny didn't notice. I'll run over and give it to Susie."

"No," Mimi said. "You always do that, Amy. You always pick up after them, begging them to notice you and approve of you. I won't let you do that anymore."

"It's just a handkerchief," Amy said, although she knew what Mimi had said was true. Amy was always trying to get Jenny and Susie to like her, and they never seemed to.

"It is just a handkerchief," Mimi said. "Pick it up, Amy, and bring it here."

Amy wasn't sure why it was better for her to bring Mimi the handkerchief than to give it to Susie, but she did what she was told. Jenny and Susie didn't even notice her as she followed them and rescued the delicately embroidered piece of cloth.

"Thank you," Mimi said, taking the handkerchief and wiping the soles of her shoes with it.

"Mimi!" Amy gasped. The once clean and lovely handkerchief was now smeared with dirt. Not even Hannah would be able to clean it.

"Your turn," Mimi said. "Those girls are not worthy to clean your shoes."

Amy took the handkerchief. It was ruined already, so it wouldn't hurt to do what Mimi said. She bent down and cleaned her shoes. It might have been wicked, but it felt good.

Mimi smiled at Amy, and Amy smiled back. "I enjoyed doing that," Amy admitted.

"Of course you did," Mimi said. "You'll enjoy what you're going to do tomorrow even more."

"Tomorrow?" Amy asked. "What am I going to do tomorrow?"

"Jenny will be wearing a new shawl," Mimi said. "Trimmed with Belgian lace. Naturally she'll be very proud of it."

"It does sound beautiful," Amy said. "Just the sort of thing I wish I owned."

"You will own it," Mimi said. "Jenny will leave it outside after lunch."

"How do you know?" Amy asked.

"Jenny is careless," Mimi said. "She doesn't appreciate what she owns, and she doesn't deserve such lovely things. Pick up the shawl and hide it in the hollowed-out oak tree. Jenny probably won't even realize it's gone until she gets home. By then you'll have taken the shawl home with you, and it will be yours forever."

"Do you really think I should do that?" Amy asked. "It seems wrong."

"No more wrong than ruining this silly handkerchief," Mimi replied. "And you admitted enjoying that."

"I'm still not sure," Amy said. "Isn't it stealing?"

Mimi shook her head. "I would never tell you to steal," she said. "You're simply going to find something that a careless girl left behind. You have as much of a right to it as she does. More, because you deserve lovely things and she doesn't."

"You're right," Amy said. "I do deserve it. I'll do just what you say."

"I knew you would," Mimi said. "You always will, won't you, Amy? We're friends for life, and you'll always do what I suggest, because I

161

will tell you to do only what you want to do in your heart."

"In my heart," Amy echoed.

"In your heart," Mimi said, lifting Amy's hand and putting it on her heart. "In our hearts, Amy. For what is in your heart is in mine as well."

CHAPTER 5

Jenny Snow came to school the next day wearing a beautiful new shawl trimmed in Belgian lace. She showed it off to all the girls, who oohed and ahhed and begged to try it on.

Amy watched with amusement. Soon that shawl would be hers, and Jenny would never know what had become of it. Mimi was right. It was what Jenny deserved, showing off all the time and being careless with her possessions. She was the same as Susie. If Amy had dropped a handkerchief, she would have known it right away and picked it up. But Susie didn't care, and neither did Jenny, and they both had a lesson to learn.

At lunch Amy sat by herself. Sometimes she and Beth ate together, but a lot of the time Beth preferred to eat alone, since Amy was frequently joined by her friends. But today it was easy to keep to herself, since the other girls were still surrounding Jenny and her silly new shawl.

Jenny gave one of the girls permission to try it on. As she did, Jenny and Susie walked over to Amy.

"Amy March," Jenny said. "You haven't said hello to me all day."

"Hello," Amy said.

Susie giggled. "Don't you want to see Jenny's shawl?" she asked. "Usually you want to see everything we have."

"I've seen shawls," Amy said. "I've seen Belgian lace. I'm sure it's a lovely shawl, Jenny. I don't need to touch it."

"But Amy," Susie began, seeming positively offended at Amy's lack of interest.

"It's all right, Susie," Jenny said. "I'm sure Amy will be chasing after us soon enough."

Amy wanted to say something back, but Jenny had a point. Until Mimi had entered

Amy's life, she had always chased after them. But Mimi was her true friend, a friend for life, and she would never need Jenny or Susie again.

The school bell rang. "We're going to be late," Susie said. "Come on, Jenny."

Jenny escorted Susie into the schoolhouse. The other girls followed them in. Even the girl who had been trying on the shawl ran into the school, leaving Jenny's coveted possession carefully folded on the ground.

Amy walked over and picked up the shawl. It was just as Mimi had said. Jenny had been careless. Now Amy took the shawl and hid it in the hollow oak tree. With a smile on her face, she entered the school. The shawl was as good as hers, and Mimi was right. She deserved to own it far more than Jenny did.

Amy dawdled at the end of the school day, then urged Beth to walk home without her. When she was sure no one was around, she went back to the oak tree and pulled out the shawl. She sandwiched it between two books so that no one would notice it and began the walk home.

Amy worried all the way, sure that Jenny would see her and know she'd taken the shawl. But Jenny and Susie were nowhere to be seen, and for all Amy knew, they hadn't even realized the shawl was gone. Maybe Jenny didn't really like it, Amy thought. Maybe she wore it only to show off how rich she was. People like that didn't deserve to own beautiful things.

Still, Amy walked faster than usual and looked around far more than she ever had. But nobody saw her, or cared if they did, and she reached home with the shawl safely in her possession.

Meg and Jo were already in the parlor, Meg sewing and Jo reading. They looked up and smiled.

"How was your day?" Meg asked.

"It was all right," Amy said, trying to keep from laughing. "Where's Beth?"

"Poor Bethy," Jo said. "She got home before we did, and Marmee dragged her to pay a call on Aunt March."

"It was her turn," Meg said. "I went last time, and you the time before that, and Amy the time before that."

"Still, she looked like a startled fawn," said Jo. "I hope Marmee doesn't make them stay too long."

"I need to go upstairs," Amy said. "To put my books away. I'll join you in a moment."

"We look forward to it," Jo said. Amy suspected she was teasing, but she didn't care. Not with a best friend like Mimi.

Somehow it didn't surprise Amy to find Mimi waiting for her in her bedroom. "I thought you might be here," Amy said, silently admiring Mimi's pale gold silk dress. "I know I hoped you would."

"Where else would I be?" asked Mimi. "You are my friend for life, and this was my first chance to see you today."

"And to see the shawl," Amy said, pulling it out from between the books. "Look. Isn't it beautiful?"

"Try it on," Mimi said. "I want to see it on you."

"Do you think I should?" Amy asked.

"It's yours," Mimi declared. "You found it, and it belongs to you. Now put it on and let me see."

Amy did as Mimi told her. The shawl was

soft as butter against her bare arms. It was dove gray, and Amy just knew it looked beautiful on her.

"You were born for beauty," Mimi said. "It's a waste for Jenny and Susie to own such things."

"Do you think I ever will?" Amy asked.

"You can have whatever you want," Mimi said. "It's there for you to own. You simply have to take it."

"The way I took the shawl," Amy said, twirling around in it. "Oh, I have to see myself."

"Where is your mirror?" Mimi asked.

"Not in here," Amy said. "We have only one, and Beth never uses it, and I haven't in a while. Meg had it last, so it's probably in her room."

"Get it," Mimi said. "I want to look at you looking at your reflection."

Amy went into Meg and Jo's bedroom and searched for the mirror. But if her sisters had it, they'd hidden it someplace.

"I can't find it," she said, returning to Mimi.

"Ask them for it," Mimi said. "They'll know where it is."

Amy went to the head of the stairs and called down. "Meg, Jo, can you tell me where the mirror is?"

"I have it down here," Meg said. "Do you need it now?"

"Yes," Amy called back. "I need it right now."

"I'll bring it up in a moment," Jo said. "Though I can't think what you need it for."

Amy returned to her room. "My sisters are like that," she said. "They have no respect for me."

"You'll have to show them they should respect you," Mimi said. "Just as you showed Jenny and Susie."

"That's right," Amy said, letting the shawl drop onto her bed. "I think it bothered them that I didn't fawn all over them today."

"Go get the mirror," Mimi said. "Jo's coming up the stairs."

Amy smiled and went to her bedroom door. Sure enough, Jo was there, mirror in hand.

"One mirror for Miss Amy," Jo said. "What do you have to look at that's so important?"

"None of your business," Amy said, trying to take the mirror from her sister.

"Not so fast," Jo said. "Meg and I both want to know." She peeked into Amy's bedroom. "What's that?" she asked, pointing to the shawl.

"Nothing," Amy said. "It's just something I found today."

Jo walked right over to Amy's bed and picked up the shawl. "Christopher Columbus!" she said. "This is beautiful. And it looks new. Do you know who lost it?"

"What difference does that make?" Amy asked. "I found it and it's mine."

"No, it isn't," Jo said. "We'll give the shawl to Marmee. She'll know what to do."

"The shawl is mine!" Amy cried. "Give it back."

"No," Jo said, and began walking out of the room.

"What's going on up there?" Meg called.

"Amy found a shawl," Jo called back. "Or maybe she stole it."

"I did not!" Amy shouted, trying to grab the shawl from Jo's hands as the girls moved back toward the staircase. "Give me back that shawl!"

Suddenly Amy became aware of Mimi by

170

her side. "Push her," Mimi said. "Push her down the stairs. It's what she deserves for taking your shawl from you. Push her, Amy. Push her!"

Jo stood with her back to Amy. She seemed not to hear Mimi, but Amy could. "Push her!" Mimi kept saying. Her beautiful face had contorted with rage, and her pale gold dress seemed to blaze with flames. "Push her down the stairs! She has your shawl. She must be punished. *Push her!*"

"No!" Amy screamed. "Stop it, Mimi! I won't!"

"You won't what?" Jo asked, turning around to face Amy. "What are you talking about?"

"I won't push you, I won't!" Amy said. "No matter what Mimi says."

"Mimi?" Jo said. "Whatever is going on?"

"Don't you see her?" Amy asked. "Mimi is right here."

"There's no one here," Jo said. "Who is this Mimi you're talking about?"

Amy looked around. She and Jo were alone. Totally alone.

172

"It was Mimi," Amy said. "Mimi made me take the shawl."

"Mimi," Jo said, the shawl still in her hands. "Who is this Mimi?"

"Me," Amy said. "Me." She burst into tears. She knew there was no point in looking for Mimi. She would see only herself in the mirror, and at that moment Amy dreaded the sight.

EPILOGUE

Jo March stood up and stretched. She'd spent the whole day in the attic, not even stopping to eat.

But she'd done what she set out to do, written the stories she meant to write. It was a long day's work, but a good one.

"Jo! Are you coming down for supper?"

"I'm coming," she called back. "I'll be down in a minute."

Jo thought about the stories she'd written. Usually she shared her work with her family. But she wasn't sure they would care for these tales.

Quickly Jo tidied her desk, carefully covering her writing. No one had to see what she'd accomplished. She'd save the stories for a cold winter's night, when the world was in darkness and when, if you listened carefully, you could hear the sound of ghosts crying in the silence.

ABOUT THE AUTHOR OF
PORTRAITS OF LITTLE WOMEN

SUSAN BETH PFEFFER is the author of both middle-grade and young adult fiction. Her middle-grade novels include *Nobody's Daughter* and its companion, *Justice for Emily*. Her highly praised *The Year Without Michael* is an ALA Best Book for Young Adults, an ALA YALSA Best of the Best, and a *Publishers Weekly* Best Book of the Year. Her novels for young adults include *Twice Taken, Most Precious Blood, About David,* and *Family of Strangers*. Susan Beth Pfeffer lives in the town of Walkill, New York.

A WORD ABOUT
LOUISA MAY ALCOTT

LOUISA MAY ALCOTT was born in 1832 in Germantown, Pennsylvania, and grew up in the Boston-Concord area of Massachusetts. She received her early education from her father, Bronson Alcott, a renowned educator and writer, who eventually left teaching to study philosophy. To supplement the family income, Louisa worked as a teacher, a household servant, and a seamstress, and she wrote stories as well as poems for newspapers and magazines. In 1868 she published the first volume of *Little Women,* a novel about four sisters growing up in a small New England town during the Civil War. The immediate success of *Little Women* made Louisa May Alcott a celebrated writer, and the novel remains one of today's best-loved books. Alcott wrote until her death in 1888.